BRIANA AND THE SAXON WARRIOR

Simon Tozer

◆ ◆ ◆

Briana and the Saxon Warrior by Simon Tozer

First Published 2019.

Third Edition.

www.devonauthor.co.uk

Cover photo by Adrian Moran.
Author photo by Poppy Jakes.

Proof reading by Peter Clarke.

ISBN: 9781095761090

PROLOGUE

Part of Dumnonia (now in modern day Devon) 656 AD

A fire burned in the hearth in the middle of the hall, with a large iron pot suspended over it on an a-frame, gently cooking a stew which filled the hall with aroma. Although there were multiple signs of habitation in the hall, only one man was inside, sitting on a vast wooden chair.

"Christos, is it ready?" The tall man with long flowing auburn hair, who asked the question, was bedecked with fine furs and trinkets and therefore must have been someone of wealth and power.

The taller of the two Celtic priests who stood before him answered "Yes, my Lord but we have not had chance to test it yet."

This was something that worried his companion Sion, he didn't really understand The Book and the power it contained and he would have preferred more time for himself and Christos to spend with it before presenting it to Geraint, their Lord and master, who was seated before them now. However Geraint was very impatient, especially since the rumours had grown about an imminent invasion. Also Christos seemed to have an unnatural confidence about The Book and what it could achieve, so Sion followed along with his companion's plans.

Geraint spoke "We have no more time, the Saxons are coming

and we need to understand the military power that the Romans wielded in order to help us defeat these vermin who steal our lands. Can your book do what I asked and show us how the people of Rome conquered the world?"

"We think so my lord. It contains the wisdom of all the writings of the priests of Dumnonia, we have also managed to make use of the wisdom of the pagans of Greece, Rome and the far off Orient." He looked sideways at Sion, both men were worldly wise and knew that there was knowledge which abounded beyond their shores and they were not afraid to tap into it.

Their priests had placed many pieces of Geraint's gold and silver into the hands of sailors and traders who brought back almanacs, treatises and studies from throughout the known globe (and beyond) to the shores of Geraint's realm. These tomes had been used to develop The Book which somehow seemed to have absorbed the information and taken on a life of its own.

Christos motioned towards Sion, who unwrapped the blanket from The Book he had placed on the crude wooden table, revealing ancient writing on the cover, which almost seemed to be alive.

Christos said "Sion take the blade."

He turned to Geraint. "Sire, we must tie the power of The Book to you, we will take a little of your blood and bond it with The Book so that it will answer only to you and your kin."

Geraint nodded his assent and pulled back his sleeve to reveal his forearm.

A shout came from outside the hall. It was quickly followed by more shouts.

Geraint ignored this and nodded again, Sion took his arm and made a small cut. Christos opened The Book to the first page which was blank.

Sion turned Geraint's arm over, hovered it over The Book and the first drops of blood dripped onto the page. When they hit the page the drops of blood spread, revealing hidden words of some ancient script which meant nothing to Geraint.

Again there were more shouts from outside, this time more anxious and then the sound of metal on metal. All three men looked towards the door but back towards The Book again, to see the words which had glowed with the blood of Geraint, had disappeared once more.

Geraint became more concerned about the tumult from outside but turned once more to Christos. "We have no time priest, what should I do?"

Sion was the one who answered "Clear your mind sire and then ask The Book what you need."

Geraint nodded once more and turned back to The Book, just as there was a rustle and crash from outside and in came two tall, blond-haired, Saxon warriors.

"Cutwulf!" shouted Geraint.

The taller of the two men smiled and made straight for Geraint with his sword and the Briton only just managed to parry the initial advance. The two men exchanged sword thrusts and parries. Geraint was aware that the second blond warrior had headed for the two priests who were doing what they could to evade him and protect themselves, Christos seemed to be using a length of wood against the warrior's sword. However at that moment Geraint was more concerned with dealing with his own aggressor.

A lunge from Cutwulf enabled Geraint to make a side -step which sent Cutwulf temporarily off balance. Geraint flashed his blade across Cutwulf's face and it made a searing cut from his nose across to his left cheek.

The Saxon warrior clutched his hand to his face and looked unbalanced. It seemed only a matter of time before Geraint would finish off Cutwulf. However there was a crash from beside him and he watched in horror as Christos stumbled past him with blood flowing richly from his throat.

Geraint turned to see the second blond warrior who, having dealt with Christos, was now standing over a stricken Sion who had already suffered one cut to his arm. The blond warrior raised his sword to deliver the mortal blow which would see off the second monk. However he never delivered the blow as Geraint wasted no time in striding across the room and sinking his blade deep into the ribs of the, no longer smiling, Saxon.

Looking at Sion, Geraint saw the priest's face turn from victory to horror as he felt metal sear into his own body.

His reflex action made him spin around and thrust his elbow into Cutwulf's face and he saw the Saxon stagger backwards and fall, while thrusting his blood covered hand out to try and stop his descent. However, the Saxon's hand only managed to find the large book which was still lying open on the table. For a moment he seemed to be steadied but then the blood spread once more across the page, showing even more writing. This time however Cutwulf's hand seemed to shimmer and then suddenly his hand, arm and the rest of his body were stretched and pulled to disappear into The Book.

Suddenly everything became still and silent.

Then Geraint himself staggered and fell to the sound of a cry from Sion of "My Lord!"

Blood was spilling from the blade wound in Geraint's back and he visibly paled before Sion's eyes.

Sion looked towards Christos but could not tell whether he was alive or dead, his attention returned once more to Geraint, who spoke.

"Take The Book Sion, take it to my son, he should have it."

Sion nodded. "Yes my lord".

"Protect The Book and my family with your life Sion."

"Yes my lord", and with that, Geraint's eyes saw no more.

Sion turned back to check on Christos…

CHAPTER ONE

South Devon : modern day

It was a typical teenage girl's bedroom. There were music posters on the wall, including some bands that Briana had never actually heard of, let alone heard, but she knew they made her look cooler than she was. There was a computer tablet in the corner, a television in another corner, clothes on the chair and on the floor. Oh and of course a teenage girl lying on the bed.

Rain played lightly on the window, signifying another grey and wet day in South Devon. It was March, so a bit of wet was fair enough but not when you were thirteen years old, had nothing else to do and wanted to go out side hang out with your mates.

Briana was thirteen years old, would be about 5 feet tall if she was standing up, rather than lounging on her bed and you could easily make out her dark, lustrous hair behind the e-book reader which was inches from her face.

The book she was reading was about a boy who started life working as a servant in a kitchen but ended up being a king and mighty sorcerer. Briana wasn't aware of this last bit yet, as she was only part way through the first book and there was a series of books. However Briana wasn't stupid and knew the boy in the book was destined for greater things.

Sometimes she wished that she was destined for greater things too or at least more than her fairly humdrum life.

This wasn't quite true. Briana was lucky in many ways. She lived in a glorious part of South Devon, within easy reach of Dartmoor and the seaside. She had some great friends and a loving mother. What she lacked and missed most though, was her father. Briana's father had died of a heart attack when Briana was just 5 years old.

Briana's Mum had tried to make up for this by being a mother and a father to the girl but sometimes, despite all her efforts, she wasn't quite enough.

Today was one of those days. Briana was feeling grumpy and sulky. It was raining outside. Her friends were unavailable. Plus she had just had a blazing row with her mother about school.

Briana wasn't the best student. She was very clever and if something came naturally to her, she excelled. However if she had to spend time working on a subject, she often found something more important to do. Just like now, she should be doing her geography homework but she was too busy enjoying her novel.

Earlier, Briana's Mum had come in with a letter from school, indicating that Briana had not been doing some of her homework. At first it had been one teacher but soon it was quite a few and it had come to the headmaster's attention.

Briana's Mum had been very angry and ended up shouting at her daughter, before storming back downstairs. Briana hoped she stayed down there.

CHAPTER TWO

The sun was setting over the ocean, the sea was azure and the beach was made up of tiny dark pebbles. A lone man sat on the beach and looked into the sun setting over the horizon. Normally he would be enjoying the view and the setting but something had him disturbed.

For those that would recognise such things, the cut of his hair and the coarse cloak he was lying on, would indicate that he was a Celtic monk. However there was no one else anywhere in sight to make this assumption. In fact there would be no one in sight for a very, very long time.

So obviously it wasn't the company (as there wasn't any) which was making him uncomfortable, so what was it?

Was it the azure sea?
No, not really, that was perfectly beautiful and he had enjoyed looking at it before.

Was it the black pebble beach?
No, again he had enjoyed sitting on these dark volcanic rocks many times in the past to enjoy the view. Plus the beaches around here were normally made up of black pebbles, so it wasn't that either.

Was it the sun setting over the ocean?
No, that sun would be enjoyed by so many for millennia to come.

Therefore, it must be the volcanoes which were erupting behind him and sending lava towards the beach?

No, he would be gone long before the lavas reached his position and anyway that again was normal for this time and place. The whole planet was erupting more than a teenager's face.

So what was it?

It must be The Book and the...

...he fought for the right word....

...people... within it, who were getting stronger. Two names came to mind immediately but there were others and it had been so long since anyone from the family had been to see him, he felt that his and their power over The Book was weakening and that worried him.

He couldn't risk those other people getting too strong.

So what was the answer?

A little girl, with flowing red hair. came into his mind. She wouldn't be a little girl any more of course but she would need to come back in.

Sion would have to do something about that...

CHAPTER THREE

Ysabel stood over the sink in a pensive mood. She had rubber gloves on her hands and her vibrant red hair tied back to stop it getting in the way.

She wasn't Ysabel to everyone of course, to her Father she had been "Darling", to Briana's friends and teachers she was Mrs Taylor, to her husband she had been "Izzy" and to Briana she was just plain "Mum". But she had been christened Ysabel and to the rest of the world, that was her name. Well it would be if they could spell it.

From the early days of school, she had got used to the boredom and frustration of explaining it was "Ysabel" with a "Y". This comment was usually followed by blank incomprehension on the part of the listener and her name being written down as Isabelle or one of the many other variations. Even when someone did finally get the point of the "Y" they often got confused with the number of "E's" and "L's".

Ysabel (as was Briana) was a family name that had been passed down for generations from her Father's side. This was a tradition that was very important in her family and one she was pleased to carry on, despite the spelling dramas it caused.

Her Father was now dead, having died a few months ago of cancer. Ysabel had been distraught as she was very close to her Father but she was no stranger to heartache. Her Mother had died when Ysabel was just a little girl and her husband had died when Briana was only a little girl as well.

At the time, this had left Ysabel in a difficult position. She had left work to have Briana and now had to sustain their lifestyle with just her income. Then Briana had started school, which was useful, as she could go to work while Briana was at school and pick her up on the way home.

She got a job as a legal secretary and her boss was really helpful by giving her the flexibility to work around the school schedule. She would have liked to progress to take law exams and become a solicitor herself, but her life around Briana just didn't make that possible.

Then when Briana got a bit older and could look after herself in the evenings, she got a part time waitress job in a local vegetarian restaurant. Sometimes with the tips, she earned more than a full day at work in Solicitors, although it was tiring and quite anti-social hours.

With these two part time jobs, Ysabel was able to bring up Briana herself and act as a mother and also a father at times. Life wasn't easy and she had to work hard to get by but she and Briana had each other, their own house and some very nice friends nearby.

However today Ysabel was unhappy. She hadn't dealt with the letter from school very well and had allowed herself to get angry and vocal with Briana. She knew the girl had it in her to do well at school and she wanted the best for her but she wasn't sure how to help her or make her do it.

That was the big question. Should she force her to do better (as her mother would have done) or nurture her (as her father would have done)?

So what could she do?

There was no point getting Briana a tutor. For one thing, she couldn't afford it and secondly, she was not sure that would work with Briana anyway.

Ysabel was frustrated that she couldn't get through to her and wondered if a father would make any difference. Derek, her husband, would have supported her but he was no longer here and there wasn't anyone else she could think of.

Ysabel was alone, her father and Derek's father were both dead and as an only child, she had no brothers to help her either. Of course there were lots of cousins out there but she didn't really get to see them any more and most of them would be of no help whatsoever anyway.

Suddenly a thought popped into her mind, as if from nowhere.

Her thoughts came back to The Book and Sion.

Sion had helped her when she was a child. She and her Father had some fantastic times in The Book but then there had been that incident in Galilee and after that she didn't trust The Book fully and what lay within those pages.

Yet it was an opportunity that most families could only dream of having and now seemed to be one of those times when it could make a difference.

The girl needed to improve at school and there seemed to be only one way to do it.

Ysabel headed up into the loft and after a little while of searching, she brought down with her a large package wrapped in an old linen sheet. She started to unwrap...

CHAPTER FOUR

Briana was sitting on her bed and looking out of the window when she heard her mother's voice. She immediately changed her expression to show that she was strong and haughty and not to be subdued.

Ysabel entered the room and tried not to look disdainfully at the mess on the floor and some of the more lurid posters on the wall...she failed.

"Briana, I need to talk to you."

"You just don't understand me Mum."

"Yes I do. You might not believe this but I was a teenager once too..." Briana looked at her mum with a mixture of incomprehension and ridicule.

"...and I was probably even more obnoxious than you are. Yes, I was a complete pain in the bum for my parents." Briana couldn't help herself from sniggering.

"But that doesn't mean you can get away with being a prize prat my girl. I want the best for you and am going to help you to achieve but it will mean hard work and effort from you too."

Briana looked back blankly and displayed no emotion.

Ysabel continued. "I'm going to give you a great opportunity but it has its risks and we're never quite sure what will happen."

There was still no reaction from Briana.

"My father had a very similar conversation with me, though I was a bit younger and I didn't know what to do with it at the time but there were some amazing experiences to come."

She continued.

"Now I want you to taste a bit of what it is to be part of our family."

Finally Briana joined in the one sided conversation.

"What do you mean Mum?"

Ysabel took a very deep breath and said.

"That you are Briana ap Ysabel, latest in a long line of heirs to the ancient Kingdom of Dumnonia and while our lands may be long gone and the title means nothing anymore, there are still items which have been passed down from generation to generation which are part of your birthright and I want to start sharing with you now."

She took another deep breath.

Briana sat on her bed and looked at her mother in wonder. The words she had spoken were not part of her normal vocabulary, they were so alien and crazy and yet, she seemed completely in earnest.

"Well, would you like to see part of your family history?" She said.

"We are descended from ancient Kings?" Briana asked.

"Sort of. They weren't called Kings in that time but our ancestors were the most powerful people in the area at the time. At various times they ruled different parts of what we now know as Cornwall and Devon, plus bits of Somerset and Dorset and even parts of Wales and Brittany on occasion. Unfortunately the English came and conquered most of our lands, so some of our people escaped to Brittany and Cornwall but our family decided to stay on. Initially they carried on fighting or standing their ground but in the end they stayed out of the way near Dartmoor and we are still here today." Ysabel replied and as she did so, she spread her arms to indicate the house, the area and the fact that they were here.

Briana looked thoughtful, the stories she had been reading in books came back into her mind.

"So do we own lots of land?" She asked hopefully.

"No", replied Ysabel. "Our family lands dwindled over time and the last farm on Dartmoor was sold by your great-grandfather about 90 years ago."

Briana looked slightly disappointed but not beaten yet, the tale of the young boy in his latest book came to mind "Do we have special powers?"

Ysabel smiled. "No, sorry we are just ordinary folk just like everyone else but we can trace our family back further than most."

Briana frowned. "Then can we call ourselves Kings or Lords, are you Lady..." she thought for a moment "...Lady Ysabel?" she concluded.

Ysabel smiled once more. "There is one man who still calls me that but no, the titles we held were all long before the advent of the English and their peerage. They would mean nothing now anyway."

Briana was now looking sullen. "So what good is it? Do we have any treasure or gold?"

Ysabel shrugged. "No, not really. Most of our ancient wealth has long been spent. Our family kept certain things from those earlier times and the most important thing is this book." She indicated the large book she had brought in with her.

She was not sure why but Briana felt a shiver run down her spine, as if this was the most important thing in her life, but in reality her Mum was just showing her a big old book. Admittedly it was probably the biggest book Briana had ever seen, even her Mum was struggling to hold it, but it was still just a book...wasn't it?

As well as being big, it looked like it had seen better days. The outside of The Book seemed to be made of a fabric which was stained and frayed. The writing on the cover was indecipherable and the pages themselves no longer appeared to be white, if ever they had been.

Ysabel looked from The Book back to her daughter and said, "this book was created back in the time when our family were rulers. It was made by a team of monks who had studied the ancient's lore and had been given knowledge which doesn't exist anymore. Our ancestor, Geraint, and the main monk, Christos, laid down their lives in defence of this book. Then it got passed down through to the son of Geraint and from him down the generations to me and now finally to you."

"What is in The Book Mum?" Briana was now becoming interested.

"It contains the knowledge, not only of the people who wrote it originally, but also the knowledge and experiences of everyone who has read and interacted with it since. There are some that think that it even gleans the knowledge of those who are yet to hold The Book. So as you can imagine, it is a powerful book and one not to be considered lightly."

"So what can it do?"

"You can find out information on pretty much anything you would like just by asking a question"

"What kind of information Mum, it sounds just like Athena?"

Athena was an online encyclopaedia, which everyone seemed to use nowadays to find out the information they wanted.

Ysabel sucked through her teeth, slightly put out that her daughter had compared her amazing book to something that people used every day.

She decided to bite her tongue and said "A bit. But also a lot more – can you talk to Athena and she will answer you?" She slowly placed The Book on Briana's bed and opened it at the first pages, which seemed to be blank.

Briana wasn't really paying attention "Duh. Yeah. Mum, have you never used the Athena app? Of course you can talk to her about anything. Though sometimes she doesn't quite understand our English accents and tells us about something totally different, which often is even better than what you wanted to know in the first place."

Briana smiled conspiratorially to herself and seemed to imagine or remember something quite naughty that she came across by accident.

Slightly exasperated at having her fire quenched by a teenager who didn't really listen, Ysabel grabbed her daughter's hand and pulled it towards the opened pages of The Book.

"Can Athena do this?" She cried

She placed Briana's and her own hand on the empty pages and all went black...

CHAPTER FIVE

Briana and Ysabel's hands were still on the pages of The Book but The Book was no longer on Briana's bed but on a small, plain table. Briana looked around herself. They were no longer in her bedroom but were surrounded by blackness. The floor (if there actually was one) was black, the sky was black and everything around them was black. In fact you couldn't tell where the floor, sky and everything else started because it was uniformly black. The only things that broke up the blackness were Ysabel, Briana, The Book and the table.

Briana looked worried.

"Wh-wh-where are we Mum?"

Ysabel smiled and said "We're in The Book Briana and there is no need to worry."

"In the what? And don't worry!"

Ysabel put her arm around her daughter and said. "I've been in here many times before and so had your grandfather and his father before him. We've entered The Book which is what we all call this book and it has a long history with our family. Oh and here comes Sion."

She indicated towards a figure who was approaching out of the blackness.

"Sharn? Who's that?"

"It's spelled S-I-O-N but pronounced a bit like SHAHN and he is the keeper of this book for our family. Hello Sion, long time no see."

"My, my dear Ysabel you haven't changed and this must be young Briana, looking like a fine young lady now."

He spoke with a lilting voice which could have sounded a bit like Welsh or Westcountry but wasn't quite either. He wasn't any taller than Ysabel and was dressed in a brown robe. His hair was cut in a Celtic tonsure which marked him out as a monk (though Briana wasn't to know this).

Briana wasn't quite sure whether she was supposed to reply or not but her Mum came to her rescue.

"Yes, Briana is growing up and it is because of her that we are here once more Sion. She's having problems with some of her schoolwork and I thought you might be able to help."

Briana was surprised at this comment, she wasn't quite sure how this strange man, who appeared from nowhere (apparently within the pages of a book, though she still wasn't sure about that) would be able to help her with her homework. Was he a teacher? Or a scientist? Or something else altogether?

"So Briana, you need to find out some things from The Book?"

Again, just like Ysabel, Sion seemed to pronounce the capital letters of "The Book" when he said it.

Briana blinked and replied "I'm not quite sure."

"Well I am sure we can help you, young lady. " Sion smiled, he looked at Ysabel before asking Briana."What subject are you having trouble with?"

Sion thought for a moment, there were a few lessons but one stood out. "Geography" she replied.

"And what was the problem? Wasn't it easy to follow?" Sion asked kindly.

"No, we have been doing plate tectonics." Briana mumbled.

Ysabel smiled "Ah yes, I never understood that either."

Sion looked enquiringly "Well of course all of that was discovered long after my time but I think we will be able to help you a bit with it Briana."

He touched the top of The Book which rustled its pages and opened at a page with lots of writing on it.

"Of course if you just read about it, you will never understand," said Sion "But if we see it happen..." He clicked his fingers and suddenly they were standing on the Planet Earth but either they were huge or the planet was much smaller than normal. Briana's foot pretty much covered the island of Sicily and she moved to stand on Northern Africa. She wondered whether she was crushing small people and trees below.

As if he heard her thoughts, Sion said "Don't worry you won't damage anything with your feet but I'd stay on the land if I were you, get yourselves steady as we're going to move in a minute."

Briana and Ysabel shuffled their feet, until they were more comfortable.

"So, this is the world as we know it today but it hasn't always been this way." Sion started to slowly move his hands. "The earth is made up of plates which move around the planet over time and created the continents as we would recognise them but many years ago..."

He clicked his fingers again and the land masses moved so that Ysabel and Briana had to hold on to each other to prevent themselves from falling over. After a few moments of moving the land masses became huddled together and covered an area of about thirty yards from North to South and about fifteen yards across.

"...all the continents were grouped together in one super continent called Pangaea, as you can see beneath your feet. I'm standing on what will become Great Britain..."

Sion pointed to his feet in the centre of the North of the super-continent before he pointed towards the feet of Briana and Ysabel just South of him.

"...but you two are on Northern Africa. However if we walk this way..."

He motioned them to turn around from where they were standing.

"...we travel down through Africa and here..." they had now reached the centre of the Southern part of the continent

"...we reach Antarctica which was much further north and not nearly as cold. You will also be surprised to see that these two areas are Australia and India!"

He indicated towards the East and South coast away from Antarctica.

Briana and Ysabel looked slightly puzzled. "India next to Antarctica and Australia?" Questioned Ysabel.

"Yes, in those days India was much further South, well most of it, some of it is right up there." Sion pointed to the top of the land mass. " Would you like to see how India moved and the Himalayas were formed?"

"Yes please" said Briana, who was becoming interested

"Could you please give me a hand Briana? I am afraid you are going to have to get your feet wet." As Sion said this he jumped off the edge of India and into the sea up to his ankles. "We are going to have to pull a bit first, Briana grab on to Tibet, I'll get Kashmir and then pull!"

Briana did as she was told and slowly some of the land started to come away from the rest, as they pulled, other landmasses started to swirl around them and connect and disconnect.

Briana noticed that some of the other continents would move one way and then the other.

Sion shouted over the sound of continents moving through the oceans.

"Over many millions of years, the continents move around and often change direction as the plates beneath them move."

Sion and Briana were moving further away from South Africa and Australia now and another landmass was swinging around towards them. Ysabel followed their progress up the East coast of what would later become Africa.

"Get around the other side Briana and push." Called Sion as he moved anti-clockwise down the West coast of India. Briana followed his lead down the East coast and started to push.

"Now when we reach the other land, don't stop!" Called Sion.

So Briana braced herself for the impact that was about to come. The sea began to be pushed this way and that as the land masses came together.

Suddenly there was a crash as India hit the land ahead. Both India and the land it had hit, started to crumple up and mini volcanoes came alight like indoor fireworks. More and more, the land folded itself up and the volcanoes raged with lava flows changing the shape of the land. Where the lava reached the oceans, the sea hissed and steamed. After a short while the activity calmed down gradually and snow began to appear on the hills that had been created.

"And that is how the Himalayas were formed. They are still rising today, as India has still not stopped its upward progress into the Eurasian landmass, though it is moving so slowly that we don't really realise it is happening." Sion explained.

"Would you like to see why the plates move around and make all this happen?" He continued.

"Yes please" said a panting Briana, looking at her Mum for confirmation, she nodded.

"No problem" said Sion, who was not sweating or breathing heavily despite the exertions of moving a whole sub-continent.

Sion clicked his fingers once more and suddenly a whole section of the earth and sea rose up in front of them, showing a cross section like a giant slice of pie. The slice ran from the crust right down to the core of the earth.

"As you may know, although we don't know exactly what is down there, the core of the earth is incredibly hot and the area between it and the crust of the earth, on which we dwell, is largely molten rock. Now molten rock will move just like any other liquid and hot substances rise. So the hot molten rock rises from the core and when it reaches the crust it starts to cool and descend again. If you look..."

He pointed to the cross section.

"...you can see how the hot rock is rising here..." he then pointed to the left of the cross section which was in the Indian ocean. "...and makes its way along the crust and drops down here..." this time he pointed to the part of the cross section which is directly below the Himalayas.

"...and that is why the Indian plate is being dragged towards the Eurasian plate. When the two plates collide, the crust has nowhere else to go and becomes crumpled up very slowly forming the Himalayas, which are still rising slowly even now, many millions of years after they started to form."

Sion looked at them both. "There are lots of different plates moving in different directions and that is why the results are different all over the world and also why the landscape of the world is ever-changing. When you throw in weathering, erosion and changing sea levels, the look of the planet will never, ever look the same again. Does that make sense?"

Briana and Ysabel nodded.

Sion continued to show them similar examples and it all became much clearer in Briana's mind, Ysabel also found clarity where before there was some confusion.

CHAPTER SIX

"So, do you understand plate tectonics a bit more now Briana?" Sion looked towards the young girl.

Briana was a bit caught out but replied "yes, it is so much easier when you see it like this."

"Even I get most of it now" said Ysabel.

"Excellent" replied Sion. "Was there anything else?" He looked at Ysabel, who shook her head.

"Then I will take leave of you both. It was a pleasure to meet you Lady Briana and I look forward to making your acquaintance again soon." He turned to Ysabel.

"A pleasure as always my lady, do not be a stranger for so long next time."

Ysabel smiled, as Sion clicked his fingers once more and all went black. Then Briana felt as if her whole body was being pulled away from her feet, until they were once more back in her bedroom.

Ysabel and Briana were sat once more on the edge of Briana's bed, with The Book open before them. They looked at each other and Ysabel was interested to know what was going through her young daughter's mind. However she said nothing.

"Mum, who is Sion?" Briana said feeling a bit more confident once more.

"Sion was one of the monks who created The Book for our family, many many years ago and long ago he made a pact to protect The Book from within. Without Sion, The Book wouldn't be safe for us to enter. Without us, Sion wouldn't have a book to belong to. We need each other and we are tied to each other."

Briana continued to look questioningly at her mother.

So Ysabel said "would you like to know more about how The Book came to us?"

Briana nodded.

CHAPTER SEVEN

Part of Dumnonia (now in modern day Devon) 656 AD

The hill could be seen for miles in every direction. It had been used as a place of refuge even before the Romans had come.

The Romans brought peace and in their time the fort on the hill had been used for keeping livestock or an overnight stop for some travellers, while the ordinary people lived in the valley below.

But now times were different. The Roman legions had long gone and the Saxon tribes have taken over the South East of Britannia and were beginning to spread further West. So the hill had once again become a place of refuge for the local people.

In other respects, things were just like they had been for hundreds of years, the people worked the fields; kept cattle, sheep and goats; made pots from the local clay and baked fish from the local rivers.

The roundhouses on the top of the hill were a mixture of old and new and were surrounded by a wooden palisade atop a ridge. Beneath the ridge were ditches and another lower palisade, newly repaired.

The hill (or dun as it was known locally) was more crowded than normal, as together with the regular residents, Lord Geraint and his small entourage were residing in the hall.

Lord Geraint's family had been chiefs of the area for a long time. Long before even the Romans had come to Britannia.

An ancestor of Geraint, called Colm the Bold had come down from the hills of Dartmoor and routed the local Chieftain in the low lands back in the mists of time. His descendants had grown stronger and ruled over much of South Devon in alliance with other Celtic Chieftains and they had become known as the Dumnonii.

When the Romans had come, things hadn't changed that much for the Dumnonii. The Romans brought their legions to Isca but the Dumnonii saw that an alliance with these new people was better than fighting and they largely got left to do their own thing.

In fact the Romans made their lives even better, as the new roads became an additional way of transporting stock in conjunction to the traditional waterways and seas, which had been used for hundreds of years. The new markets in Isca and the trading post at Milber became handy repositories for the goods of the Dumnonii and they grew more powerful.

When the Romans left, things didn't change that much for the Dumnonii except that they now collected the taxes and kept them, rather than passing on to the Roman officials in Isca. They also continued to worship their Christian god, just as they had done in the times of the Romans.

So the Dumnonii grew richer and their lands grew but then the pagan invaders started coming from across the seas. At first the effect on the Dumnonii was minimal but then other Romano-British people started coming from the East, displaced by the incomers.

Then as the newcomers conquered the East, warriors came West to join the Dumnonii and they fought great battles against the Saxon invaders and they were successful all over the South and

West of Britannia.

Then more people came from Germania over the sea to Britannia and the incursions became more frequent. The Dumnonii had no fears of being conquered but the raids on their livestock were damaging and recently the invaders had been after gold and jewels too. One particular Saxon had been causing more trouble than most recently...

Cutwulf was a sixth generation West Saxon. His three times Great-Grandfather Wulfric had left Friesland 170 years earlier and sailed to East Anglia, where he had joined his cousins from Friesland and then they had headed Westwards, battling for land with the resident Romano-British.

Wulfric's descendants had slowly moved West and helped make Wincaester their stronghold. Cutwulf's grand-father had moved even further West but been repelled at Durnovaria by the remnants of the Durotriges and their Dumnonii allies. Ever since, Cutwulf's family had made sorties into Dumnonia but were unable to take any more land.

All that changed with Cutwulf, who had proved to be a great, if somewhat unpredictable, leader. He still followed the ways of Woden, unlike some of his contemporaries who had switched allegiance to the Christian god and when his two eldest sons were killed in battle with the Dumnonii, his hatred of these British had grown and his desire to kill the chieftan who had slaughtered his sons, Geraint, had become an obsession.

Against the advice of his trusted inner circle, he decided to lead a near suicide mission into the heartland of the Dumnonii and even now was closing in on Geraint's hill fort.

Inside one of the roundhouses, two men were leaning over a table which had one item on it. A book the size of which had not been seen before by any of the people of the village. In fact most of them rarely saw a book at all, because none of them could read.

Both of the men could read but that was not surprising, as they were both priests. The Celtic church was still strong in Dumnonia in the 7th Century and, unlike the Saxon Kingdoms, there was no influence from Rome here, they knew when the true date of Easter was and they cut their hair in the true Celtic tonsure. Also, thanks to Christos, they had the benefit of ancient wisdom that their Latin and Saxon counterparts knew nothing about.

The fruits of some of this wisdom was sitting on the table in front of the two men. In truth, it was the taller of the two men who was key to the success of the project. The shorter priest was just an instrument of his brilliance. The shorter man wondered where Christos had learned about the possibilities of The Book but when he questioned the taller priest, he just got the answer "divine wisdom is sometimes passed down to us lesser mortals Sion."

Sion's family were closely related to that of Geraint and he was also a direct descendant of the great Chieftain Colm who had come rampaging from his ancient hill fort on Dartmoor when things had become too difficult to survive up there.

Sion's family had always been in the higher echelons of Dumnonian society and in Roman times they had run the trading post at what would later become Milber and also the smaller staging post at Dain, nearby to what would later become Ipplepen. It was here that Sion had spent his early years before joining the church across the sea in the land of the Bretons.

He had recently returned home to the land of his birth shortly before the arrival of Christos, who was helping to change everything.

Where Christos had come from, no-one knew. He had arrived on a boat in the port of Saltcoomb in the South and offered his

BRIANA AND THE SAXON WARRIOR

allegiance and wisdom to the Dumnonii against the invaders. He spoke many languages including Breton, Latin, Greek, Aramaic and even some of the languages of the new Saxon invaders.

He was taller than everyone they met, even Geraint who was considered a giant among his people. His skin was darker than the majority of people he encountered and his wisdom seemed to be the strongest of all. He often spoke of things that made no sense to the Dumnonii and he had introduced some amazing new devices that even the Romans had not known.

However his greatest achievement was to be The Book. How he had come to create it, no one knew but they did know it was going to be something special.

Sion secretly wondered whether The Book had nothing to do with divine intervention but was actually a pagan marvel wrapped in Christian clothing but their need was strong and he didn't question Christos too much. He was fairly sure his Lord didn't care at all, all that mattered to Geraint was protecting his people and lands from the Saxon invaders.

Christos spoke to his companion. "Shall we go in now?"

Sion said "if you are sure?"

The taller man nodded his assent, picked up The Book and they left the smaller hut. They made their way to the main hall and nodded at the two sentries who stood either side of the doorway.

CHAPTER EIGHT

Ysabel told Briana all of this and also how Cutwulf had slain Geraint but then become absorbed into The Book.

"So is Cutwulf still in there?" Briana asked

"Yes, his power comes and goes but he is inside there and he hates our family for what we have done to him, killing his sons and then enslaving him in the pages of The Book."

Ysabel looked intently at her daughter.

"What is it?" Briana said

"Nothing much, I was just wondering how you were feeling?" Ysabel asked.

"Fine." Came the short reply. Briana was actually not feeling that happy, whereas when she was in The Book, she realised she had felt alive!

While she was in The Book, everything just seemed RIGHT. Capital letters are very important sometimes in getting a message across and now was a perfect example. It was just RIGHT.

She didn't know why but everything seemed natural and even more real when she was in there. Perhaps it was The Book, perhaps it was being with her mum, perhaps it was Sion or maybe a combination of them all. She wasn't sure. Now she felt that a joy was leaving her, life wasn't as much fun as it had been just a little while before.

Ysabel continued to look at her daughter.

"I know what you are thinking, as I've felt it before and am feeling it again. You want to go back into The Book because that is where you feel at your best. Being part of The Book feels like the most natural part of your life and now that you are back in the real world you are missing it. Am I right?" She looked at Briana partly in a quizzical way, partly knowingly.

Briana nodded her head. "Yes, can we go back in?"

Ysabel looked deeply at her daughter before replying.

"Yes but not straight away, we need to overcome this feeling so that it doesn't overpower us. If you give in to the power of The Book it can destroy you. Members of our family have been sent crazy or been overwhelmed by The Book in the past and we need to make sure that doesn't happen to you or me."

Briana began to look frightened.

Ysabel looked at her daughter and continued in a soothing voice.

"Don't worry, we can manage it if we are sensible. That is why we don't use The Book all the time, because it can take over your life and some people have been lost to The Book and never returned."

Briana looked even more frightened. "What? You mean that The Book killed them?"

Ysabel shook her head. "No. They didn't die exactly. What I am really talking about, are those people who lost the will to return to the real world and become part of book itself. Some were turned crazy, so we don't want to encounter them and others become so integrated into the pages of The Book, you would never know who they are. Then there are the...others."

"Others?"

"The Book only works for people from our family, it is tied to us by blood, so that no one else can access it unless we take them in with us. However there is Cutwulf of course, plus some members of his family have sometimes got in too. Then there are some members of our own family who have turned bad. So there are some bad people in there that we need to be careful of, as they hate us and all of our family. I will tell you the story of one other lady in there but not today, I think that is enough for today."

Briana now looked really scared. The desire to rush back into The Book had rapidly waned.

Ysabel again looked at her daughter with gentle concern and said in a soothing voice.

"Don't worry, as long as we use The Book sensibly and always stay with Sion, we should be fine."

Briana was looking quite thoughtful. She had experienced a whirlwind of emotions and enlightenment over the past few hours and now she didn't quite know what to think. Her mother continued...

"The Book is a blessing bestowed on our family but we just need to treat it with caution and then we can enjoy an amazing resource for experiences and education. I tell you what, we'll have something to eat and then a quiet night and then go back in tomorrow. If you would still like to?"

Briana was less sure than she was but the desire to go back into The Book was still there, plus she couldn't imagine what they would see next. So she nodded her assent.

"But you need to keep it to yourself for now, so don't mention to anyone else. Ok?" Ysabel said.

Again Briana nodded her agreement.

"Ok let's go and have some tea and we'll start thinking about what we will try and do in there next time."

Ysabel put her arm around her daughter's shoulder and led her out of the bedroom.

CHAPTER NINE

West Wales (modern day Devon and Cornwall) AD 1067

His long hall, which was made of stone, would have put to shame many of the dwellings of the English Kings in Winchester, Wilton and London but Caradoc could no longer field an army of Britons like some of his ancestors had done.

Only a few generations ago, the English had purged the British from the port of Exeter, a city they had held power over on and off ever since the Romans had left, but now it was in the hands of the English once more.

Caradoc himself had been forced to swear fealty to Redver, the Saxon lord who held dominion over this part of Britannia. If he hadn't, he would have been isolated even more and would have lost what little power he still held.

In fact they no longer called it Britannia, the name England was now being used for this realm. Caradoc and his cousins were some of the few who would still think of themselves as Britons, as the native peoples had become integrated more and more with the Germanic and Norse invaders and evolved into the English.

Even Caradoc's cousins down in Cornubia were now under the thrall of the West Saxons who had emerged as the most powerful people in England.

Now, however, there had been a complete change. The English had been defeated by the Normans at the battle of Hastings and Caradoc saw an opportunity to claim back some of his lands from the English invaders, who had seen many of their best men slain in the battle.

Caradoc himself would have been at the battle if he had not been laid down by an ague which had seen him with a fever for over a week. So he had stayed at home with the women and children, waiting for information on the battle for nearly a month before it all became clear what had happened.

Harold Godwinsson, who claimed to be King Harold, had defeated the Norsemen at the Battle of Stamford Bridge in the North of his realm, only to hear that William the Bastard of Normandy had invaded in the South. Marching his men South in just a few days, the tired Saxons had nearly routed the Normans but the battle had turned and the men from across the channel had been successful and wiped out a generation of English fighters and lords.

Caradoc knew only a little about the Normans but felt that they could be little worse than the English. Their battles to maintain a new large Kingdom might enable he and his cousins to take West Wales once more and return it to British control, just as they had managed to do briefly a hundred or so years ago.

If the Normans succeeded in subjugating the English, it would take them time and this time would allow Caradoc to show his power and sue for a treaty. They would surely be happy to treat with a strong leader who would pay them in gold and look after their Western borders.

Caradoc envisioned himself as ruler of all of West Wales (stretching from Cornwall to the mouth of the Severn river) in alliance with his British kinfolk in North Wales and Brittany, who he still traded with by sea. Perhaps one day they would join together and see the English, Danes and Normans banished from their shores once more, as they returned to the power that the British had managed under the Romans.

So Caradoc dreamed, as he sat in his stone hall.

However, in reality, these were all pipe dreams. For although he could still raise a small army and perhaps ally himself with other Britons, the chances were they would not look to him to lead them and he had another concern, his son.

His son did not have the fire of his father and ancestors. He was well read and a great studier but the men would never have followed him into battle, if it had not been for influence of his father. Caradoc had tried to train the boy and cajole him into becoming a great warrior and leader but it seemed he was not destined to be one.

He just wished that his other child had been born a boy as she would have lead them to glory. The girl was the one with the fire and spirit.

Morwenna looked at herself in the mirror of polished brass and was pleased at what she saw. She was taller than most women, with an athletic body that many men would be proud of, yet she was still a fine figure of a woman that men found attractive.

What irked her however, was the sword at her side. It was not the sword itself, for that was one of the finest in the country. No, it was what the sword meant. If she had been a man, the sword would have been a sign of high status and would probably already have seen some major action. However Morwenna was a woman, so the sword at her side was little more than an adornment, a sign that she was from noble and warrior-like lineage but not a sword that was to be used in battle.

This was a perception that Morwenna had spent most of her young life trying to overturn but had not succeeded much. One of the most formative events in her life had occurred when she was just fifteen and her brother Tristan fourteen.

They had both gone out on a boar hunt, Morwenna without her father's knowledge, with a group of their father's warriors. Having become detached from the main group, they had searched the woods and valleys in search of their prey.

Then suddenly a mighty crashing sound had come to them from further up the valley. They both knew what this meant and got themselves ready, with their spears held firmly in their arms and legs braced.

A boar from hell had suddenly appeared crashing through the undergrowth. It must have stood four feet tall and with tusks which could cleave through a man's body.

As it came at them, Tristan tried to spear the boar but only received a shoulder barge and was lucky to have been missed by the boar's huge tusks. Morwenna however, waited till the last second as the boar went straight for her, she danced aside and swiftly brought her spear down on the boar's exposed neck. The boar gave a tremendous roar, stumbled and then started running again. It crashed on for another twenty yards before stumbling to a halt.

Morwenna rushed up to its side, placed her hand on its shoulder for a few moments and muttered a quick eulogy to the boar, before gently putting it out of its misery with a knife cut to its neck. Finally she removed the, now broken, spear and rested her hands on the boar's side once more.

It was a fine beast, who had died well and deserved to be treated with respect. Her brother came crashing through the undergrowth towards her, took in the scene and said, "Morwenna, that was amazing. Father will be so pleased."

Morwenna glowed with pride.

They trussed the boar's legs together, tied it to Tristan's spear and grabbed one end each to enable them to carry the dead boar.

Tristan took the lead and Morwenna followed behind, looking forward to the reception and reaction from her father and his warriors on her success in killing her first boar.

It took them about an hour to return to their home. Most of the warriors were already back and were bustling around the courtyard, cleaning swords and spears but they all stopped to watch the two youngsters coming through with their trophy.

Word must have spread quickly as, before they could get much further, their father came striding into the courtyard. He took in the scene, his son leading the pair of them, battle scarred and carrying a dead boar on his spear and Caradoc liked what he saw.

"Tristan my son, you have defeated your first enemy and you will be rewarded with a great feast where we will eat this magnificent beast." He roared.

Tristan, bemused turned to his sister before looking back at his father and started to say "but Father, it was..." but he got no further as Caradoc overwhelmed him in a big bear hug saying, "I am so proud, my son."

Morwenna looked on in bemusement and hurt but knew it was only a matter of moments before the truth would out.

She started to say "Father, it was..."

At the same time Tristan tried once more "Morwenna was..."

But their father cut across them once more to call out to his warriors. "Look at my son the warrior. Isn't he fine? Colm and Evan. Take the beast to the kitchens so that they can prepare it for the feast, while my son and I return to the great hall of our ancestors where he can now sit with pride and honour."

Two of the warriors came and took the boar from Tristan and

Morwenna. Tristan was led off to the great hall by his father and Morwenna was left feeling alone and confused.

That evening her father held a great feast in Tristan's honour, lauding his hunting prowess and blessing the beast which had given its life for his son's glory and to feed the whole group.

Tristan sat in bemusement and shock. He had tried to explain the situation but the more his father lauded his achievements, the harder it became. After the feast he tried to explain this to his sister but she got even more confused and angry and decided to walk away from her brother.

What had happened? Her moment of glory was taken from her and her brother had been made into a hero in her place.

From that day on, things changed in the family. Caradoc favoured his son in everything, training him to become a warrior and lord. While Morwenna was pushed to the sidelines and reserved for dealing with the female side of things.

She and her brother barely spoke any more, although they did spend time together, Tristan was almost too embarrassed to bring the subject up and increase the ire of his sister.

Morwenna continued to train for fighting and any of her father's warriors who were foolish enough to take part in trial combats with her, soon found out that it was not a good idea, as they were likely to lose and there was no benefit to be found in men who suffered defeat at the hands of a mere woman.

Her father laid out a plan of marriage for her to some Saxon Lord and Morwenna could only hope that what she heard was true and that these Saxons treated their women as equals and that he would be proud of her prowess, rather than treat her as a mere chattel.

She also began to dream of using his fyrd to conquer her father's lands and take her rightful place at the head of the family here in West Wales. She knew she had the power and strength, her brother would be brushed aside and as for her father she would look on in delight as he realised that she was the great warrior in the family and not her bookish brother.

Caradoc was still dreaming of greatness while he waited for his children to come before him. After a while they arrived side by side.

Tristan was now a young man with long, dark hair and dark eyes. He carried a large book under one arm and had a sword sheathed by his side.

Morwenna was now a young woman with bright, auburn hair and long blue dress. She was as tall as her brother and her equally dark eyes, showed a determination that would shake most men.

Caradoc looked at them both in turn and addressed the boy first. "Tristan, my son, bring The Book to me, it is time for us Britons to take control of our country once more. You shall fight and stand by my side as is your right."

Tristan nodded his assent and delivered The Book into the hands of his father, who turned to the girl.

"Morwenna. Tostig Sigurdsson is dead, killed in the English rebellions that occurred after Hastings, so you will no longer be wed to him. Instead I will wed you to one of our British cousins from the West or over the sea to make an alliance."

Morwenna looked stricken. She was the eldest child who should by rights be leader of her people but her father favoured Tristan and was blind to her power and potential. However she had seen a marriage with Tostig Sigurdsson as a welcome match and opportunity to take back what was rightfully hers. A match with one of her Celtic cousins would not work so well. She had depended on this alliance with this West Saxon.

Then the damned Normans had come and upset everything. Tostig had survived the Battle of Hastings and had raised an insurrection against William of Normandy but his fyrd was weakened by battle, illness and inexperience. Obviously her father had recently heard news about his failure and death (which had not yet reached Morwenna) and decided on a new path for her.

She knew that she would be married off to someone who would be tied by treaty to her father and later her brother, which would mean a life of inconsequence and misery for her.

She had the fire of her ancestors in her blood and it would not do to have her wasted on the sidelines while her weaker brother had all the opportunity and glory. She knew that she was wiser, stronger and more practical than either her father or brother.

She had to act quickly if she was to do anything about it.

Tristan was talking to Caradoc "Father, have you consulted The Book and Sion about how best to deal with the Normans?"

Caradoc smiled. "Boy, we don't have to defeat the Normans yet. We just have to take back control of our own lands and the Normans will be happy to treat with us as neighbours. Their realm will be large enough for now and they won't be able to fight everyone." Holding up The Book he said "the monk knows nothing about modern warfare and politics, his ideas and information are tired and a waste of my time."

Morwenna's eyes flashed with inspiration, as she thought to herself. If she had The Book and her father's throne, the power could be hers once more. She didn't trust the monk Sion but he held knowledge and power which was far beyond the realms that others could muster and if she was the guardian of that power, who knew where that could lead her?

Morwenna made a decision.

She watched as Caradoc handed The Book back to Tristan, who took it in both of his hands. As her brother was otherwise distracted, Morwenna took the sword from the sheath by his side and walked to the throne with her father on it, he looked at her with confused eyes before saying.

"Child, what are you doing?" His quizzed look turned to horror as she pointed her sword towards his chest.

"I'm no longer a child Father but a strong woman." She said and turned to her brother.

"Tristan, give me The Book."

Tristan looked on at her in confusion.

So she repeated once more.

"Tristan, The Book." As she said this she nudged the sword at her father once more and gesticulated towards Tristan with her other hand indicating that she wanted him to give her The Book.

"What are you doing child?" asked Caradoc.
Then Tristan started to walk towards his sister with The Book.

Caradoc got to his feet and called out "Tristan, no!" But as he did so, he stumbled over his own long gown and fell forward, directly onto the out-stretched sword that Morwenna had held at his chest.

The sword buried deep into his chest and blood almost immediately seemed to gush from his astonished mouth down the sword and over the hands and body of Morwenna, who stared dumbfounded at her father and then at the sword in her hand.

She struggled to pull the sword out and was concerned that her brother would attack her but he was standing open mouthed in fear and incredulity and he dropped The Book in his confusion.

Morwenna watched The Book drop and reached to pick it up. However as soon as she placed her bloodied hands on The Book it turned from russet brown colour to flaming red and the heat emanated from it like a furnace.

She tried to let go but her hands are almost melted into The Book and she couldn't do anything but drop the sword. She screamed in pain as The Book turned from red to white and suddenly her whole body melted and she was sucked as one into The Book which tumbled to the ground.

Tristan was left standing, his mouth agape in a state of shock.

His father was slumped in his chair, blood was still flowing from his wound and mouth, though that was the only movement from his body.

Tristan's sister was gone, presumably into The Book but not in the normal way that they entered to learn about the ancient wisdom of their people, with the guidance of the priest Sion. No, she had been pulled in the most violent way he had ever seen and with such pain in her eyes, he would almost feel sorry for her if she had not just killed their father.

He knew that he was now the leader of his people but his shock at how it had happened would haunt him for the rest of his life. He placed his hand on The Book and called for Sion.

CHAPTER TEN

Briana knew nothing yet of all of these events in her family history which had happened nearly a thousand years previously. She was just a regular Twenty First Century Devon schoolgirl who had all the normal things to worry about and get excited about.

However, today she had one special thing to be excited about and that was returning to The Book again and she wondered what they would do next. Her mum had mentioned a couple of ideas but said they would talk about it more this evening.

Now she was lying in bed. For some reason she was wide awake even though it was only 6am. She didn't have to get up to get ready for school for ages yet.

Suddenly her Mum came in through the door gesticulating.

"Why aren't you up yet? It's swimming practice this morning."

Briana groaned. What with all the excitement with The Book, she had completely forgotten about swimming.

"Do I have to Mum?" One look at her Mother's face, gave Briana all the answer she needed .

"Yes of course you do. You know there is a big gala in a couple of weeks and I know you enjoy it."

Briana looked a bit glum. "Yes but coach is a real bully."

Ysabel's gaze softened slightly. "That is the nature of swimming coaches Briana, they are there to torture young children, just as they were tortured before by their own coaches. It is the only way that we are trained to become upstanding British people, who can also swim a bit!" She cracked a smile as she said this last bit.

She looked at Briana who wasn't sure if she was joking or being serious.

"Coach isn't really a bully, she just knows she has to keep you all working hard in order to get the best out of you. Be honest, if she wasn't hard on you, you know you wouldn't push yourself quite as much would you?"

She looked at her daughter who shook her head and mumbled something which sounded a bit like "S'posenot"

"Good. If you ever really want to pack in swimming, I won't make you do it but if you want to swim in the galas, you have to train and that means getting up early before school."

She looked at her daughter with tenderness.

"You do want to swim don't you?"

Briana took a moment before nodding.

"But why do we have to get up so early?"

"We're not the earliest group, there is another group who start an hour before us. That would mean getting up at 5am."

"Ok."

"Swimming is important. It is something you enjoy, something you are good at and it is also how your father and I met, when we used to swim against each other at galas across the South West of England. Then we went and did the summer life saving down at Bantham beach together. Oh I remember the parties we had in the sand dunes. Those were the days."

Briana knew she would have to get her mother away from

reminiscing or else she would be off on a memory trip for ages.

"I just thought that with The Book, we wouldn't have time for things like swimming any more."

Ysabel smiled. "We don't stop our lives because The Book has come into them. Like I said, swimming is important. You never know when swimming could save your life."

Briana scoffed. "How is swimming going to save my life?"

Ysabel looked serious. "Let us hope you never have the occasion to find out."

CHAPTER ELEVEN

A man was feeling happy but slightly unfulfilled. He knew he was stronger than he had been for a long time and he wanted to use that strength to get some revenge.

The problem was that he hadn't seen any of Geraint's family for a long while, even that damned red-haired girl who thought she was something in here.

He needed to end that family's line for what they had done to him and his sons but his last opportunity back in ancient Judea had proved fruitless. He had come so close to ending that line of British vermin and also the potential side bonus of changing the course of Christianity but ultimately he had failed.

He was also concerned about that damned monk, who seemed to be able to stop him most of the time. Well that British fool couldn't do it every time and now he felt strong enough to defeat the monk too.

He looked around at his surroundings.

Anyone interested in physics could have told him he was inside the nucleus of a hydrogen atom but to him it looked dull and featureless. It was also not likely to be a place of opportunity for his requirements.

From somewhere a glint caught a scar on his left cheek. "Cutwulf, I think I need to be somewhere else" he said.

CHAPTER TWELVE

Despite the arguments, swimming had been a great success and Briana was confirmed as the freestyle swimmer in her age group for the upcoming South West of England competition. So that made it an even better day.

The rain was still coming down outside and, even though it was March, the weather felt more like November or December. It seemed to be getting dark, even though it was only 6pm.

As there was little else to do, Briana was helping her mother in the kitchen. For a girl of 13, she was surprisingly adept at cooking and happy to get involved. This was because her mother had got her enjoying joining in with the cooking at an early age after her father died, as a way of bringing them together. Also, as they were both vegetarians, it was a good way of teaching her to cook for herself, as it was always harder for veggies to find good food compared with omnivores.

Today they were making a vegetable curry, Briana was crushing and mixing together the fresh garlic, coriander, cumin seeds, cinnamon and turmeric with coconut milk for the sauce, while her mother was frying some butternut squash and potatoes in some already sautéed leeks and celery. When the vegetables were nicely beginning to caramelise on the outside, Briana poured the well mixed sauce into the wok and it sizzled violently for a moment, while Ysabel stirred the mixture until it started to bubble gently.

She then turned the heat down really low and started the rice, which Briana had already rinsed thoroughly and into which she would later add the lime and lemon-grass dressing she had made just before. The cooking was now managing itself, so they continued their conversation from earlier.

"What would you like to see in The Book next?" Ysabel asked her daughter.

Briana looked unsure. "I don't know, what can we see in there?"

"Practically anything you want, as long as there is a section on it in The Book. We can either just open up The Book and look through the pages or if you are not sure what it might come under, we can just ask Sion to find it for us."

Briana stirred the curry and, enjoying the aroma, thought out loud. "How about where all these spices come from?"

Ysabel looked brightly at her daughter, nodded and said "yes, that is a great idea. I'd love to see that too. We'll do that after dinner."

CHAPTER THIRTEEN

How long she had been in there the woman didn't know, time didn't mean much in The Book. In fact, she looked the same as she did on the day she arrived.

All she knew was that things were changing. There were times when she was barely nothing and could not influence anything but at the moment she felt strong, stronger than she had felt in a long time.

She remembered that previous time when she had felt as strong as this, some pestilence was striking the outside world, the family were nowhere to be seen and it was some time before The Book was used again.

She hadn't taken full advantage of that situation at the time, as she had been caught off guard. Then the family had returned to The Book and so she had missed her opportunity. But now she was strong and ready, so she just needed to be in the right place at the right time.

Where was she now?

A dull landscape without any colours. The rocks were grey and and there seemed to be no vegetation.

She looked up into the sky and it seemed to be night-time but wasn't that the sun over there?

And what was that blue green planet over in the other direction?

Realisation began to dawn on the woman. She now knew where

she was. She was in a very cold place but the fire for revenge still burned strongly within her.

From her location on the moon, she spoke to no one in particular. "I think I ought to get away from here and have some fun. Sons and daughters of Tristan, Morwenna is waiting for you!".

CHAPTER FOURTEEN

Back on Planet Earth, Briana and her mother had gathered together in Briana's bedroom once more. The Book was still lying there, on her bed. As it was so large, it filled up quite a bit of the bed's surface.

Briana started to study it properly for the first time. The cover was fairly plain but there did seem to be some writing on it, which seemed to appear and disappear as Briana moved her head. It also did not seem to be using any alphabet that Briana could recognise. The pages themselves were barely visible with The Book closed but there did seem to be a lot of them.

Ysabel picked up The Book and opened it up at the first page. "Are you ready?" she asked Briana. The girl nodded.

"Then you do it." Ysabel proffered The Book towards her daughter.

"What do I do?" asked Briana.

"Take my hand, then place your other hand on the page and ask the question."

"What question?"

"What you would like to be shown."

Briana did what her mother said. She took her mother's left hand with her own right hand and at the same time placed her left hand on The Book and said out loud "show me where the curry spices come from."

Just like before, the room went black and then there were swirling lights and the feeling of rushing wind. This time the lights went green and bright before they found themselves standing in a new location.

All their senses seemed to be bombarded at once.

Their ears heard a gentle cacophony of bird song, insect calls, flowing water and also some indistinguishable mammalian calls.

Their noses registered the heady earthy smells of forest, roots, branches, leaves and flowers. Together with unknown sweet perfumes and fragrances.

For their eyes, they found themselves in a tropical paradise with verdant trees awash with trailing vines and flowers glittering everywhere. There were birds flying through the branches and the sky was blue, with the sun shining down through the canopy of leaves and branches, creating little shafts and pools of light.

The heat was immediately apparent to their skin, along with the moistness in the air, heightening their sense of touch.

Finally, they could actually taste the air, spices and rich honey like pollens were distinctly tangible in the light breeze.

Briana had never been anywhere like this before and even for Ysabel the experiences were beyond what she has seen, heard and felt before.

Briana wiped her brow as she took in the wealth of sense sensations which bombarded her mind. She didn't know where to look or what to do first. She was like a kid in a sweetshop overwhelmed with the wealth of delights on offer to her.

"Where are we Mum?" She finally asked.

Ysabel smiled and looked around. "I don't know, but I like it!"

Her eyes glistened as she walked over to a tree, she gently grabbed a branch and smelled a pink and white blossom from the tree . "Delightful" she said.

"Obviously it is somewhere tropical. When you said curry, I thought of India but I don't think we are in India, although of course there are jungles in India. Sorry Briana I don't know. Ah, here we go."

Her last comment was made towards the forest as they saw Sion walking towards them through the trees. There was not much of a path and he needed to duck his head a couple of times in order to prevent himself being scratched by the tree branches.

"Hello my Lady, young Briana" he nodded to them both in successio. "Back again and so soon. And..." he looked around at their surroundings "...in such a delightful spot."

"Yes it is magical, where are we Sion?" asked Ysabel

"We are on the island of Run in the Moluccas, which were once known as the Spice Islands. At one time the islands were the only source of nutmeg, clove and mace in the world. Around this time those were the most important spices in the world, changing hands for lots of money and inadvertently will even partly lead to New York becoming a British colony but that is another story. However I thought it would be good to come here now with the height of interest in these islands and their spices."

Briana and Ysabel looked at each other.

Sion continued. "There are other islands and lands which grow spices, I could take you to India, Burma, Indonesia, Malaysia and many more. However I thought it might be interesting to be here because this one small island, as well as being home to three of the richest spices in the world at this moment, changed the course of British and world history."

He continued. "The year is 1618 and down the hill is a little

British fort."

He walked to the edge of the glade to the brow of a hill and pointed down through the trees towards a coastline set against an azure sea.

Briana spotted a wooden ship moving just off the coastline and wondered what it was.

"Is that a British ship Sion?" she asked.

Sion shook his head with a smile. "You have a good eye Briana. No that is a Dutch ship and they at the moment are the masters of the waves around these seas. They are also the reason why this island will become so important and it all is down to the people inside that fort there."

He indicated a rough path leading down the hillside in the direction of some craggy rocks atop of which there was a palisade with wooden huts inside, a few with smoke rising from the small holes within their reeded roofs.

The palisade that surrounded the fort seemed to be made of something like bamboo, Briana not being an expert in such things, was not quite sure what it was made of but it didn't look like normal wood. The palisade was about ten feet high and the path down from their hill joined with another larger one, which lead back down towards the shoreline where another ship lay. This ship was smaller and fatter than the one they had seen earlier, which was no longer in sight.

Two soldiers who looked to be Europeans stood in the gateway to the fort but they were surrounded by people who were obviously native in origin.

Sion continued.

"The fort is home to a small band of British sailors, merchants and locals. Their leader is a man called Nathaniel Courthope, it would be great to meet him but perhaps not today, as we are really here to look at the spices. However without that one man's efforts it is unlikely that Britain would have owned what was to become New York and later the United States. There is a good chance because of the events and treaties which followed the battle for Run and the other Spice Islands, that the Americans could have been Dutch speaking or something else altogether rather than English. This would have dramatically changed the direction of world history."

"However, although I thought it would be interesting to you, we are not here today to see the man but the source of the spices, which were so important."

Sion indicated a path which lead off sideways to the fort and Ysabel and Briana followed him.

The short journey was magical to Briana. Although at some points it felt just like walking through the woods at home and she was no expert in British fauna, let alone the tropical varieties, Briana knew that the plants here were a world away from what she was used to seeing at home and they filled every spot imaginable.

The trees ranged from tall giants to short and squat, with a wide variety of leaves and blossoms. Trailing from the trees were climbing plants, some with flowers and she could tell that these combined with the blossom were the source of much of the smell, which had a sweet, honey-like aroma to it.

Among the trees were a wealth of birds, many with bright plumage of all the colours she could imagine. Some were tucking into the sweetness which alighted from the flowers and blossom, others were hunting down the insect life, of which there seemed to be no end in this jungle. Briana was used to seeing insects back home and had never really paid them much attention, until she had been bitten by the odd ant or stung by a wasp.

But here they were everywhere and you had to pay attention to them. Butterflies bigger than her hands flew past beetles of every colour, which seemed to have scuttling races with the centipedes and millipedes. Giant stick insects would crawl along the branches but what really stood out were the ants, some were very large, other were smaller but all together there were so many of them. They marched across the path, along branches and through the gaps in the trees. Many carrying half eaten bits of leaf, sometimes three times the size of their own bodies.

Briana just wanted to stop and watch. She also knew there were other animals around, as she sometimes heard scuttling in the undergrowth but she wasn't able to see anything.

Presently however, they stopped in a bit of jungle which was much alike the rest of the forest they had walked through and Sion indicated in one direction.

"That tree to your left is called *Myristica fragrans* and when it grows a seed it will be the source of nutmeg and mace. Right now it is flowering and you get these lovely white flowers but soon the drupes will form and lead to the most expensive spices in the world right now, which you can only get from this island and a couple of others."

Briana looked interested.

"How much is the spice worth?"

Sion smiled. "Well, to give you an idea. The contents of this one tree, would buy you back in England, your mother's house plus quite a few of the rest of the ones in the street!"

Briana looked shocked. Even though she didn't really know how much houses cost back home, she knew that this was a lot of money.

Sion walked over to the tree with Ysabel and her daughter following him, as he did so, he gave a little twisted wave with his right hand and winked at Briana.

Briana watched as, among the flowers, what look like pears began to grow on the tree and Sion cupped a fully grown one in his hand. "My little trick." He said to Ysabel and Briana.

The pear-like item was light green in colour and as he spun it around they could see it was starting to split to reveal a conker like shape inside.

Sion gave the fruit a little twist and pulled it down to show them.

He continued. "This is the fruit of the tree but it is what is inside, which is the most important part."

He broke open the fruit just like you would with a horse chestnut fruit and a conker. However, once opened, what was inside was not as much like a conker as they both thought.

There was a nut inside which was vaguely conker like but it was surrounded by red strands meshed around the nut, almost like someone had dribbled red wax around the nut.

"Is that nutmeg?" asked Ysabel

Sion replied. "The nut inside is the nutmeg, this red lace-like substance on the outside is the mace. They can be used together but more normally you would remove the mace from the nut by leaving it in water for half an hour and then dry them both out to create the lovely aromatic spices."

He passed a couple of fruit to Ysabel and Briana who both looked at him questioningly, he nodded so they both broke open the fruit to reveal the mace covered nutmeg inside. They both sniffed them and held them for a while.

"Would you like to see the next stage?" Sion asked the other two.

They both nodded, so he clicked his fingers and suddenly they were elsewhere.

CHAPTER FIFTEEN

A man sat on a veranda wearing a red uniform. His hair was fair and there was a deep scar running across his face, the remnants of a fight he fought many years ago.

He enjoyed the power that this new role gave to him. A few tens of thousands of men controlling a country of millions, they were so powerful. Plus the climate was warm and the food, once you got used to the spices, was excellent.

However something worried him.

A feeling he had not felt for some time. Apart from a few encounters with others in The Book he had not felt challenged for a long while but something felt so very different suddenly.

He heard a noise and almost expected that damned monk Sion to appear but it was just the serving boy bringing him a cool drink.

Perhaps he didn't need to worry, perhaps the new feeling was a chance rather than a challenge. He had become a little bored over recent years.

Perhaps it could even be an opportunity to escape, something he had been thinking about more in recent years as his power seemed to grow.

Perhaps this was the chance to settle some scores which go back many generations.

A smile crossed his scarred face and he thought to himself "Cutwulf, perhaps your time has come once more."

CHAPTER SIXTEEN

Sion, Ysabel and Briana still held their nutmegs in their hands but had suddenly been transported to a busy street far away from the tropical jungle. The buildings were made of wood and corrugated iron. This was obviously a market street as each property had products on display outside, except for a few oddities, like the man on a chair who was having a shave from a barber.

The street was obviously somewhere in the Indian sub-continent, judging by the look of the people around them, and there were so many people. It was a bit disorientating after the isolation of the Indonesian forest, the street bustled with people on foot, and there were no cars to be seen.

There were, however, animals to be seen everywhere. A couple of men led a white horned cow down the street, there were a few dogs and then a troop of small monkeys bounced across the street. The people mostly ignored the new arrivals, apart from one man who threw some flowers towards them.

The people were mostly poorly dressed in robes of dirty white and brown but in amongst them were grander people in very colourful dress.

But what really hit our three visitors, was the smell. So far removed from the pleasant smells of the forest. It was nothing like Ysabel or Briana had ever encountered before. If it was just the smell of the spices (which were laden all around them on stalls) they could probably have coped but the smell seemed to be coming from everything – the people, the animals, the street, the houses, the dirty stream which ran alongside the street and the cook pots which steamed on some of the stalls and inside some of the houses.

It wasn't necessarily a bad smell, just an overwhelming smell for the senses. Briana gagged and felt like she was about to throw up as the nasal symphony hit her senses like a cricket bat pummeling a ball for six. Ysabel, who seemed to be able to cope more readily than her daughter, went over to Briana and gently rubbed her back in a soothing action until she stood up again, her eyes still watering a little.

Sion looked like everything was normal. "When you've grown up in a 6th century stockade in rural Devon like I did, you are used to most smells." He said by way of explanation.

Briana's senses seemed to settle down and she started to take in everything else around her as well as the smells. Sion walked towards a small grouping of stalls, all of which displayed sacks of spices.

"We are in Kerala in the late 19th Century. It is the days of the British Raj and India produces much of what will be exported around the vast British Empire and that includes spices. Where once you could only source mace, nutmeg and cloves from the Spice Islands, now the British have brought seedlings over to India. So India has many spice plantations and is probably the biggest source of spices in the world."

He approached one of the stalls, put his hand into a small sack and brought out a handful of whole nutmegs and showed them to Ysabel and Briana before he returned them to the sack.

He then walked to another sack and again brought out a handful of light brown powder, this time he proffered it under the noses of Briana and Ysabel who both sniffed.

Briana turned and sneezed but Ysabel smiled gently as Sion

said "that is the nutmeg, which was so prized back in the 17th century. It is still valuable by the time it reaches Europe but not as much as it was and here it is not worth very much at all and can be bought easily in every small village along with..." and he indicated towards other sacks. "...black pepper, cloves, turmeric, coriander, cumin, garam masala – which includes nutmeg – and much, much more."

Briana and Ysabel walked over to the stall and started to smell and try some of the different spices. Ysabel walked over to Sion, asked him something and he handed back some coins and some little raffia sacks.

Using the sacks and the money, Ysabel went to the stall and had many of them filled up with spices. She then swapped money for the spice laden sacks with the middle aged gentleman there. Sion passed her a basket when done and she deposited the raffia bags into the basket.

"That's our curry spices sorted for a while, we should come here more often!" She displayed a big grin as she said this.

"Would you like something to eat?" Sion said, he gestured towards a street stall with rough benches outside where locals were already eating.

"Remember that we are vegetarians." Ysabel said

"Don't worry, over half of India are vegetarians and although we are in Kerala which is less vegetarian than some parts, I've found us a very nice vegetarian option here."

He held up three fingers to the young lady who started to approach them and she headed off back to the outside kitchen. Sion, Ysabel and Briana took their seats on the benches around a larger bench and quite quickly food started to arrive. There were different dishes containing a range of spices and vegetables, some that Briana hasn't seen before. One dish was filled with rice and they also had little flat breads in a wooden bowl.

Briana looked for the cutlery but sensing her confusion, Sion pointed to another table where some of the locals were eating and said "you eat using the breads."

Briana watched the locals doing it before Sion demonstrated by picking up a bread, breaking it in half and and splitting it down the middle to form a scoop, which he then dunked into one of the bowls and started eating the food.

"Delicious!" he said and the others followed suit.

It was truly the most delicious meal Briana had ever tasted. Some of the vegetables she wasn't so sure about but there was such variety. As they ate, more dishes came to the table but as they were sharing between three of them and the bowls were small, it was just about the right amount of food.

More locals kept arriving and most sat at one large table where everyone was sharing together from the larger dishes.

"I thought we would prefer our own food, rather than sharing with everyone else" said Sion as he indicated towards their own relatively modest spread of food, which was now much depleted.

"I hope you are getting some ideas for some new dishes for home Briana?" Ysabel asked.

Briana was actually enjoying the food too much to think about cooking herself, however she nodded anyway.

"I've got the spices…" Ysabel said as she indicated the sacks at her feet "…all we have to do now is learn how to use them!"

Suddenly a disturbance was heard from a street ahead and then a group of soldiers in red uniforms came trotting through the streets. The crowd parted as they came through, the soldiers were not aggressive or did anything particular but the crowd stayed out of their way, almost as if to say "just in case".

Sion looked at his two companions. "Perhaps we should take our leave, we don't want any unfortunate questions."

Ysabel and Briana nodded their assent.

Sion left some coins on the table and they quickly headed off back towards the market and the place where they arrived. As they left, one of the soldiers, who arrived just after the other main group, stopped to watch their progress. He particularly watched Briana, as she, her mother and Sion disappeared from the street in front if him.

The soldier stared firstly questioningly, then realisation crossed his face and then wonder. He seemed disgruntled to have missed the little group but then a smile crossed his face, which was scarred from his eye to his cheek...

CHAPTER SEVENTEEN

Ysabel was a little concerned.

She had mostly stayed out of The Book for more than twenty years because of the dangers it could mean to her and her daughter but now she was engaging in it once more.

Was she right to do this?

It was fantastic to enjoy these journeys but was it worth risking their lives for?

She decided to chat to Sion about it.

He appeared immediately when she opened the inside page of The Book. He was once again wearing his monk's habit and Ysabel wondered briefly whether he got it laundered or somehow it magically cleaned itself.

"Sion, I need to talk to you."

"I wondered why you had come without the girl. That is good, as I need to speak to you as well."

"I'm worried about the safety of my daughter, it has been some time since I have been in The Book but I know there are ..." she hesitated before continuing "...people in there who wish to do harm to me and my family."

Sion nodded. "That is actually what I wanted to talk to you about as well."

He continued. "I am pleased that you have returned to The Book after this time because your family ties to The Book have been weakened by your absence and that weakening of your blood ties has strengthened the power of your enemies."

Ysabel looked confused. "What do you mean Sion?"

"The power of The Book grows every time you and someone of your bloodline interacts with it. You are tied together by the blood of your ancestor and each member of the family who has entered The Book since that day that Geraint first gave his blood to The Book."

Ysabel nodded her understanding and Sion continued.

"However I have noticed, that any prolonged absence by the family weakens these ties and plays into the hands of our enemies, who are then able to exert greater control over the stories and the dangers that they can present to us. I am even concerned that they are growing in strength to the extent that they will soon be able to break the barriers which prevent them leaving The Book."

"You don't mean that they could come back into the real world?" Ysabel sounded very concerned.

"Yes, that is a possibility and there are some people in here who should not be allowed back out again, as they would be able to wreak havoc."

Sion continued. "You have to remember that there are others in there who have very strong blood ties to The Book as well. People like Morwenna are directly descended from Geraint and others like Cutwulf have been in there since the start. It is only because The Book has been passed down from generation to generation, that your tie is stronger than Cutwulf's."

Ysabel looked worried. "How many others are in there?"

Sion in turn, looked worried himself. "I do not actually know. Some are in so deep, they have become part of the stories and probably never be seen again, others might re-awaken if Cutwulf or Morwenna, find it useful to do so. There might also be some in there who might help us if we needed it, most of your ancestors were not bad people!"

Ysabel smiled.

Sion grinned grimly. "My concern is, that unless we assert our control over The Book once more, that someone like Cutwulf – who probably understands the book more than anyone other than myself – will wrest control away from us."

Ysabel took a while before replying. "Does that mean we have to destroy The Book?"

It was not an easy thing to say but she realised that it might come to that.

Sion shook his head. "We cannot. The Book is not just the physical book but the power that we harnessed fifteen hundred years ago, combined with the blood and power of all who had interacted with The Book in the generations since. If you destroyed the physical book now, those beings inside would become corporeal once more and I dare not imagine what power they would hold or havoc they could create."

Ysabel was horrified but also slightly pleased as really she didn't want to destroy her family book. "So what can we do?"

"You must interact with The Book once more and get your daughter to do the same. Perhaps, if we pull the power back towards your bloodline it will weaken those who have become stronger in your absence."

"Is that our only option?"

Sion nodded. "I think so, if you want to prevent people like Cutwulf from cutting lose in 21st Century Britain."

Ysabel shuddered at the thought and then considered the

prospects. "Will we be safe returning to The Book?"

Sion this time took a while before replying. "I cannot guarantee anything but if you make sure you are with me at all times, I should be able to make sure you are safe."

Ysabel hoped he was right but her mind wandered back to Ancient Judea.

CHAPTER EIGHTEEN

Over the next few weeks Briana, Ysabel and Sion spent more time together in The Book and despite the worries emanating from her conversation with Sion, Ysabel found she was enjoying spending more quality time with her daughter, whilst also seeing her schoolwork improve.

A surprisingly enjoyable afternoon learning about algebra as they all jumped in and out of three dimensional floating shapes, was followed by visits to the laboratories of Davy, Cavendish and Lavoisier to learn more about Chemistry.

On this particular evening however, Briana had come home looking glum. She unceremoniously dumped her school bag on the floor and grabbed a glass from the cupboard to make up some squash. Each item was banged noisily on the worktop. First the glass, then the squash bottle, then the glass with the undiluted squash and finally the glass which became resplendent with diluted squash.

Ysabel didn't need to be a rocket scientist or a specialist in child behaviour to know her daughter was craving attention and waiting to be asked what was wrong.

Exhibiting a slight sadistic streak, she waited for half of the squash to have been imbibed before asking innocently, "did you have a good day at school?"

In return she got little more than a grunt, which sounded a bit like "ayateblodge" a comment which was incomprehensible to most people but to those who understood basic teenager, could be translated as "I hate biology".

A more understanding or less sadistic mother would probably have replied with something like "oh dear, what happened?" Enabling the child to unburden their woes on an understanding ear.

However Ysabel was not done playing her little games. "Oh dear, that's a shame, I always really enjoyed biology."

This new statement proved counter-intuitive to the teenager in front of her and elicited the meaningful response "whuh?"

Which again could be translated as "what?" or to those of the more precise English "I beg your pardon?"

Ysabel smiled a grin that was just a little bit too wide and knowing "yes, it was always one of my favourite subjects."

She looked back at Briana, who was looking at her mother as if she was a deranged harpy from some unknown world, outside of her sphere of understanding.

Having had her fun she decided to put her daughter out of her misery for now and asked her "why, what was wrong with biology today?"

Although she had got what she wanted, Briana didn't show any sign of delight or victory at the change in the line of questioning. She did however answer her mother's question.

"Bloody circulation of the blood, I don't get it and Wilson embarrassed me in front of the whole class."

Ysabel decided it was probably not the best idea to comment on her unintentional pun or his use of the teacher's surname instead of the more correct "Mr Wilson" and instead decided to make her daughter's life a little easier.

"Well perhaps Sion can help us." S said it so nonchalantly, that even Briana picked up on it, though she didn't know what it meant.

"You mean another trip into The Book?" she asked instead.

"Yes. I seem to remember doing something along the same lines many years ago. Hopefully it will help you with your school work." Ysabel managed to make this sound very sincere but underneath she was getting excited.

"Shall we go up now or wait until after tea?" Briana asked her mother.

Ysabel smiled. "Probably best if you don't eat first..." She left that sentence hanging, so that once again Briana was wary. What was she planning? What did she know about blood circulation and what would The Book show them?

With some trepidation, she followed her mother up the stairs.

For the first time in a while, her mum picked up The Book before her and had already opened it up and placed her hand on a page as she sat down. She took Briana's hand immediately and they both got pulled into The Book and presently were standing before Sion.

The monk was grinning from ear to ear. "Again, Ysabel?" he said.

"Briana is struggling in biology Sion and she needs some help with a particular topic, tell him Briana"

Sion smiled at this direct speech and looked at the young girl who dutifully commented. "Circulation of the blood, I don't understand it at all."

Sion gave a little laugh. "Of course Young Briana, I will help you with your schoolwork."

He indicated towards Ysabel. "You don't need to come though Ysabel, if it is just school work."

Ysabel rolled her eyes. "Stop messing about Sion and let's get going and have some fun."

She turned to Briana. "You are going to love this, forget about learning about the circulation of the blood and enjoy the ride my girl!"

Briana wasn't quite sure what she meant but Sion lead them both off into the darkness.

Minutes later they were squashed into a small space with some bouncy material behind them and a wall of some strange substance. Briana started bouncing rhythmically and said, "what is this Sion?"

"That is the subcutaneous fat surrounding the blood vessel we are about to enter." He indicated towards the wall in front of them.

He then took a long knife from somewhere and he cut a slice about 4 feet in length into it. He then pushed his arm through the wall and he brought back, one by one, three large red objects.

Looking at them, Briana was reminded of the tractor inner tubes she and her friends used to use for white water rafting on the river. However these were red and where the hole should have been, they were filled in with more red. They were round and about four feet in diameter, so Sion only just managed to pull them through the gap.

"Briana, we are currently just outside one of the blood vessels in the left arm. We are going to ride on these red corpuscles." He indicated the three red circular things.

"We will be taken to the heart, where the blood will be pumped into the lungs to be oxygenated, before returning to the heart and then head off to the rest of the body."

They each got hold of one of the red blood cells and followed Sion to the break in the wall.

He turned and shouted to them both over the noise coming from inside the wall.

"Ysabel you've done this before, so you go at the front, then you Briana and I'll take up the rear so I can keep an eye on you both. The main thing Briana, is to hold on tight!"

Ysabel pushed the red blood cell through the gap in the wall and jumped aboard it as she did. Briana followed suit and was immediately pulled forward as the blood cell joined a group of others being pulled or pushed through a large tunnel. They weren't moving that quickly, as the tunnel could only take two or three blood cells at a time and all were straining to go through the gap.

Briana took the opportunity to get right up on top of the blood cell like her mother had done and also turned to see Sion doing the same thing behind her.

Gradually they began to speed up as the tunnel widened and Sion maneuvered his blood cell to come alongside Briana. He gave a thumbs up to Briana as he did so. Briana nodded in response.

She could see her mum ahead but she seemed to be going slightly faster and began stretching away.

Suddenly they joined a larger vessel from the side and really started to speed up. Sion motioned to hold on tight. The blood cell felt slightly spongy to Briana's touch and because she started to be hit more by other blood cells, she was pleased that they were spongy and not hard.

They were now travelling very quickly. Sion came up alongside Briana. Briana was not sure how Sion was maneuvering his blood cell as she had no control over her own.

Sion shouted out to Briana. "Hold on tight we are about to enter the heart soon." He indicated how he was now lying down on his blood cell and holding tight with arms and legs.

All of sudden the pressure changed completely, and there was a deep booming sound which seemed to ring through their ears and their whole bodies. Briana found she had literally no control over the blood cell now as she was whooshed and pulled forward. One moment she was upside down and then turned all around, as if she was on the most exciting fairground ride ever.

One of the best things was that she felt totally safe, the other blood cells surrounded her and although they all felt like they were moving at some vast speed, she enjoyed the feel of the spongy blood cells around her. It was like riding on a roller-coaster through a ball pool!

They darted through long tube-like passageways, linking one chamber after another and then entered into the largest chamber yet. It was a large strange shaped cave with thousands of the red blood cells. Briana's blood cell shot across the cavern and then she spotted her mother rocketing past on her blood cell clinging on like a rodeo rider, when suddenly Ysabel was thrown clear and disappeared.

Briana started to shout out to her mother and see what she could do to help, only to be sucked though another hole in the ceiling and back into a tunnel. Briana found she was been dragged away from the large chamber and she turned to look over her shoulder but could see neither Sion or her mother in sight.

She started to panic.

What would happen to her mother?

Could Sion help her?

Where was Sion?

Where was her mum?

Despite all these worries, there was nothing Briana could do about it as her own blood cell was travelling so quickly, that it was all she could do to hang on.

However bit by bit, they slowed down as they moved into narrower tunnels. The blood cell slowed to a walking pace, so Briana jumped off and moved to the side of the tunnel.

Now what?

She was alone inside a human body, she didn't know where she was or how to get out. She had no mobile phone with her, so had no way of trying to get hold of her mum or Sion even if they were both conscious.

What would happen if they were both knocked out by getting thrown from a blood cell, how would she ever find them and how were they going to get out?

Could they have drowned or been crushed in the heart by the blood cells?

Would they be stuck in here for ever?

Briana resolved to start making her way back towards the heart. However, she quickly established that this wasn't going to be easy. Firstly it was quite tight with all the blood cells, which were heading in the other direction, squeezing past her. Secondly there seemed to be some force pulling her in the opposite direction, making it feel like she was walking uphill, against the wind in a sand dune.

She started to despair and when one over large blood cell crashed into her and knocked her over, she crawled into a ball hanging on to the wall of the tunnel wall and started to cry.

It was her worst experience so far in The Book and at that point she just wanted to get out.

It was here, a few moments later that Sion found her. The monk jumped from his blood cell and got down to comfort the girl.

"There, there Briana it is alright, I'm here now."

Briana looked up, wiping away the tears from her eyes "But mum, is back there, she was thrown off one of the blood cells and I don't know what happened to her".

Sion smiled kindly. "Oh. I am sure she will be OK." As he said that, he looked back down the blood vessel, just as Ysabel came around a corner riding a blood cell and whooping in joy.

Catching the view of her daughter, she jumped clear and got down to comfort Briana but her daughter still seemed in shock. Ysabel said, "don't worry Briana I am here now."

"I-I thought you'd been thrown off your blood cell and we'd lost you!" Stuttered her daughter.

"Oh bless you. I was fine. I've been thrown off before and all you have to do is hitch another ride. You did amazingly well to stay on your blood cell all the way through."

This last comment didn't really comfort Briana that much but, after a while she calmed down again.

Sion cut another hole in the tunnel wall for the three of them to climb out of.

As they got clear once more Ysabel, still flushed with exhilaration said, "well that was one hell of a ride!"

CHAPTER NINETEEN

It was a surprisingly cold morning for April and when Briana awoke, she did not want to get out of bed, especially as it was the weekend. Eventually she dragged herself out of bed and into her dressing gown, before heading downstairs.

At first she thought the kitchen was empty but she soon became aware of her mum sitting quietly with her back towards Briana.

"Morning Mum" she said with all together more gusto than she had originally planned. As she came around the kitchen table Briana was able to see that her mother had no breakfast in front of her but was holding on tight to her coffee cup. The coffee did not seem to have been drunk and she was making no attempt to drink any of it. As Briana made her way towards the fridge, looking to get some juice and yoghurt, she was able to see her mum properly for the first time.

She was looking very intently at the coffee cup in her hand and her eyes were swollen and red, showing signs of heavy crying. In fact, right at that moment a tear dropped down from her eye to her cheek.

Briana wasn't quite sure what to do or say but couldn't help herself from saying the obviously banal "are you alright Mum?"

Ysabel looked up. Registering her daughter for the first time. "Oh Briana. You're up. Would you like some breakfast?" She dabbed a couple of tears away from her eyes as she spoke.

"No, it's OK. I'll sort it" Briana replied and went to the fridge.

Briana's mother sat back down and returned almost at once to her coffee cup devotions.

Watching her, Briana wondered what could have happened to her mother? Why was she in such a state?

She tried to cast her mind back to the day and night before but nothing seemed to come to mind. Then she thought about what was upcoming and reached the same dead end. Finally she thought about the date. What was it? April 19th? Ah that would be it.

Her dad's birthday.

Forgetting the juice, she went and sat with her mother and put her arm around her.

Ysabel looked at her daughter intently, knowing that she knew. No words needed to be spoken. They just held on to each for quite some time.

After a while, Briana helped herself to some breakfast and her mum drank a fresh cup of coffee.

Eventually Briana said, "what would you like to do today Mum?"

Ysabel knew that this was quite an effort for Briana. It was a Saturday and she would probably have mates heading into town or something else she would rather be doing than hanging out with her mum.

She was tempted to say that it was all okay and she should go off and have her fun but them something stopped her. She realised that this day, of all days, should be a family day.

She knew exactly where she wanted to go and said just this to Briana.

An hour later they were both lying in swimming costumes on a Caribbean beach in the middle of the 12th Century.

"Your father and I came here a couple of times, when I told him about The Book." She smiled at the recollection.

"I didn't tell him about the whole thing. I just said that there was this special portal to this different world that we could enjoy sometimes."

She paused at the memory.

"However I think he always knew more than he let on but he didn't want to press me too much. He was always nice like that, your dad."

Briana loved hearing her mum talking about her dad. She barely remembered him now apart from little snippets but he did sometimes pop up in Briana's dreams. She could just imagine her dad now on this beach and wished he was there with them.

Suddenly she had a thought. "Mum, couldn't we..."

Ysabel interrupted her daughter before she got any further "No. We can't. Sion told me long ago, that you can't go searching for dead people who are too close to you. It upsets The Book and bounces back on you so hard that you may be lucky enough to live to regret it."

She sighed.

"No. We will just have to make do with our memories and enjoy our own precious time together." She took a sip on the drink, which they had bought with them and looked around the beach.

They were on one of the lesser Caribbean islands which was not occupied in the 12th Century. Although the Europeans would not reach these seas for another three hundred plus years, many of the islands were home to the indigenous Caribbean people.

This one however was deserted and a true tropical paradise. The sea was warm. The sand was soft. There didn't seem to be any marauding insects ready to take advantage of their pale British skin.

At that moment Sion appeared wearing swimming shorts and while he looked a bit odd out of his usual Monk's habit, Briana had to admit that he did have the figure to carry it off.

"Right" said the monk. "Who fancies a swim?"

Knowing that they were both very active swimmers, he barely waited for an answer before running into the sea. Briana and Ysabel followed him in to enjoy an excellent time frolicking and racing in the warm surf.

Briana couldn't remember spending a better day with her mum, which was quite ironic seeing as how it had started.

One of the best things about this way of visiting the beach, apart from the fact they had a long sandy beach to themselves, was the simple pleasure of nipping home for anything they wanted.

They made a quick trip back to collect lunch and Ysabel even brought a nice bottle of wine and three glasses. Sion enjoyed his glass and even Briana joined in and pretended that she enjoyed the taste.

She and Sion then headed off into the trees in search of coconuts. After an exhilarating but exhausting hour, where she tried without success to climb a tree in the manner Sion explained to her, she managed to down a coconut using rocks.

However once she had it in her hands it didn't look much like a coconut to Briana, being much bigger and green in colour. Sion explained that the brown husky nut she was used to was inside and that she would have to break it open. However a few hearty blows on a nearby rock were unsuccessful so she decided to take the whole thing home and cut it open instead.

Briana enjoyed much of the rest of the day quietly reading her novel on her e-book reader. She was still enjoying the same series of books about the tales of the young boy, who was still travelling around unaware of his greatness to be. However she had to admit that her own life was getting pretty extraordinary now. Perhaps someone could write a book about her story.

She shook her head and went back to reading, that was just a stupid idea.

After a very pleasurable day, Ysabel and Briana said goodbye to Sion and headed back home.

When they were back in Briana's bedroom once more. Ysabel turned to her daughter.

"Your dad would have been proud of you today, though maybe he would have won the swimming race instead of you!"

Briana looked back at her and smiled all the way through getting ready for bed.

CHAPTER TWENTY

Some times Briana went on her own into The Book but Ysabel insisted that she always went with Sion and never without telling her where she was going.

Briana was enjoying her time enormously but Ysabel also made sure that Briana was doing the normal things that teenage girls did, such as going dancing or hanging around town with her friends. She was sworn to secrecy by her mother but something inside Briana ensured she didn't want to share this secret with anyone else anyway. When she told her mother about this feeling, Ysabel nodded.

"It is something deep inside of us which I can't quite explain but I felt it too. I think it must be something to do with our blood ties with The Book and the way it has been passed down from generation to generation through our family. Maybe The Book has its own way of protecting itself."

Briana looked at her mother curiously, she sometimes had this way of referring to The Book as if it were a person or alive and she asked her about it on another occasion.

"The Book is special and perhaps it is alive." Ysabel replied when her daughter asked her. "It contains the blood of many of our ancestors and there are human beings who have stayed in The Book so perhaps it takes on some of their human-ness." She added "if such a word exists."

"You say there are humans in The Book. What do you mean?"

"As I said before there are some humans who go in just like us but never leave and they become part of The Book. I'm not sure they could leave now even if they wanted to. Some have become part of the stories in there, others have died in there. There are also some people who are not members of our families who are in there, though it is harder for them to get in and even harder for them to become part of The Book but some have and some are even more dangerous than some of the most deadly things in The Book."

Briana looked a little bewildered and Ysabel realised she hadn't explained it very well.

Ysabel looked at her daughter. She was just a girl but her father had told her about Cutwulf at an even younger age, as he felt she needed to know properly about the dangers The Book held as well as the delights.

She looked deeply into Briana's eyes and spoke.

"Remember I told you about Cutwulf, the man who killed Geraint, the first owner of The Book?"

Briana nodded.

"We're not sure exactly what happened but after the fight, Cutwulf ended up in The Book."

"At first our family thought that was the end of it, particularly as they were more interested in staying alive and living their own lives. But when they used The Book, they began to notice that Cutwulf was still in there and taking up different roles within sections of The Book. Not only that but he seemed to hold a vendetta against members of our family. The first they were really aware of this was when one of our family members, a man by the name of Conoc, was killed by Cutwulf while he was learning about the Trojan Wars. Cutwulf had become one of the Greek heroes and used the background of the war to kill Conoc while he was watching from the walls of Troy."

"Usually Sion can protect us, just like he did when we walked through the oceans or travelled through blood vessels but somehow Cutwulf can take control of a section in The Book and make it possible for us to be killed. But it does vary from time to time, sometimes he has just joined a story, or Sion has more power in there, or The Book itself is able to protect us in some way."

She looked carefully at Briana.

"But we do have to be wary of Cutwulf, so I want you to promise me that you will never go in without me or Sion. Promise?"

She looked intently at her daughter, who nodded her assent and said. "Of course Mum." Briana gave a little shiver as she said it, as she thought about this 7th Century English warlord who sounded very scary indeed...

Ysabel looked thoughtfully at her daughter again. "I had a close encounter once with Cutwulf, would you like to hear what happened?"

"Yes Mum!"

"Alright."

CHAPTER
TWENTY ONE

Cana, Galilee AD 30

The three people hadn't been invited to the wedding but they felt they had a good reason to be there. They looked slightly out of place compared with the people around them, as they walked through the mud-brick streets but the locals barely glanced at them.

The tall man was dressed like a local but he wore modern spectacles and very impressive sideburns, which were all the fashion back home.

The shorter man, wore a brown robe and had his hair cut in a special way and was way too fair-skinned to be a local.

The girl was quite young, about 12 or 13 and also dressed in local clothes but as he she walked, occasionally her tartan Bay City Rollers pop socks could be glimpsed beneath her robes. Giving away, not only the place she came from but the time too.

They headed towards a large courtyard where many of the locals seem to be gathered. As they entered, they could easily make out the newly married couple, who were the centre of attention.

However the girl scanned the crowd for another face and turned to her father. "Which one is he Dad?"

Her father made a "shushing" sound and walked toward an older man, who seemed to hold some semblance of power here.

"We are travellers, who have come far but would like to bless this wedding, is there any wine so we can bless the couple as is the custom in our parts?"

The older man looked at him for a moment before he replied. "There was no wine but our friend over there made sure there was, for which we give thanks." He nodded towards a tall bearded man to the side who nodded his acknowledgment back.

Her father had a mixed look on his face following these words but the girl just stared at the bearded man, as the three visitors were each given wooden goblets and liquid was poured in.

Her father raised his goblet and said "the happy couple" and drank, the shorter man and the girl followed suit. The wedding guests looked slightly bemused but copied the toast.

The girl wrinkled her nose as she drank but the shorter man exclaimed "mead!"

The taller man said "yes Sion, not really the wine we had expected but we know our man had something to do with it. Just a shame we got lost and didn't arrive a bit earlier to see how he did it."

Sion replied. "Ah Gryffyn but then the miracle may not have happened. I think it is best that we arrived late."

Gryffyn looked at Sion and wondered whether their lateness was contrived. He looked back towards his daughter but found she had walked across the courtyard and had started talking to the bearded man.

"Is your name Jesus?" she asked him directly.

"Yeshua" he replied, just as Sion and Gryffyn joined them.

Sion leant over to the girl and whispered "Yeshua is the Hebrew form of the name Jesus." She took a moment but then understood before she continued, and held out her hand.

"I'm Ysabel." Her father smiled as Yeshua took her hand between his two larger hands.

Yeshua was a tall man with very dark hair, a strong nose and tightly curled beard. His skin was almost olive in colour and he had very dark eyes.

"It is a blessing on my family to meet you Ysabel" he said before he continued. "Did you like the honey wine?" He indicated towards the goblet

"I did thank you, did you make it?"

"I? Make wine? No, I am but a humble carpenter and worker with wood but I helped in bringing the drinks to the wedding today for my brother's wedding."

He indicated towards the newly married couple. "Joses is a lucky man to have such a wife and we needed to make sure that they had something to drink to go with their repast."

"Isn't that right mother?" He looked towards a short woman with long dark hair.

"Yes, my son but I also wonder when you will be married." She looked towards Gryffyn and Sion as if looking for support but they both just nodded sagely.

"Ah, but I have much to do before I can be tied to such earthly pleasures as marriage. I am also a teacher." He looked at Sion and Gryffyn who nodded again.

"What do you teach?" asked Ysabel.

"You are a perceptive child Ysabel, you ask the questions your elders do not. What do I teach?" He looked around as if waiting for an answer, when there was none, he continued.

"I teach understanding of the ways of Yahweh, for we have lost the right path and need to find it once more."

Sion stepped forward. "I am a follower of Yahweh also, although we give him another name where I come from. My name is Sion and I would love to hear more of your teachings Lord."

Yeshua held up a hand. "I am not a lord, as I said I am a humble carpenter who has been shown the ways of Yahweh and is helping others to do the same but I would be delighted to talk to you further Sion and to your friends."

He indicated a small table surrounded by chairs which had just been vacated by some others of the wedding guests and they each started to take a seat.

However there was a shout from outside the courtyard which was quickly followed by screams.

A woman came running into the courtyard and shouted. "Pirates from Sidon have come and are killing everyone they can."

Just as she said this, three men on horseback rode into the courtyard and slashed their swords indiscriminately amongst the bewildered wedding guests.

A fourth pirate entered and surveyed the crowd which had started to get up and flee. He shouted over the screams. "Remember I am looking for two men with a small girl, I want them alive if possible but I won't shed a tear if you accidentally kill them."

Even on horseback you could tell he was taller than the others. Plus his blond hair and a scar which ran from one eye to the other cheek, made him stand out from the other pirates.

Yeshua looked at his companions as he heard these comments. He held hands with his mother and Ysabel, pushed his way through the crowd and said "follow me."

"What about your brother?" asked Sion.

Yeshua looked at his mother before he replied. "He will be fine, he can fight with the best of them." Just as he said this, they saw some of the wedding party had started to fight back against their invaders. They already appeared to have taken down two of the attackers but more were arriving.

Yeshua lead them from the courtyard, and zig-zagged through alleyways, until the tumult from the attack started to subside.

However the sound of horses hooves could soon be heard again behind them. Yeshua took a couple of sharp turns and the group struggled to keep pace with him. Ysabel however seemed to be the most fleet footed on the ever-winding narrow path of alleyways through which he led them.

Just as they thought they were escaping, they turned into another alleyway and there before them were three of the Sidonian pirates on horseback. The tall blond one was amongst them and he sneered at Sion.

"So monk, we have you cornered." He gave off a little laugh.

Before Sion could reply Yeshua interjected "I don't know who you are pirate but you have no place here in Cana."

"Be quiet peasant" shouted back the blond man.

"Cutwulf!" exclaimed Sion in exasperation. "Do you not know to whom you speak?"

"What is some Judean tramp to me monk, even if he thinks he is the son of a god? I am descended from Woden himself, who would crush this Christian god beneath his feet, just like I will do to all of you now!"

Yeshua retorted "I do not know of what you speak pirate, I am a follower of Yahweh and if you and your men get down from your horses, perhaps we can all take some wine and discuss this as men, rather than resorting to the sword."

"Enough of this prattle Christian. I only want these two men and the little girl. You are nothing to me." He turned to his companions and indicated towards the monk and the little girl and shouted "seize them!"

He himself headed towards Gryffyn.

Yeshua however stood in his way, so Cutwulf slashed towards him with his sword, missing by inches as the carpenter ducked quickly.

Yeshua's mother was not so lucky however, as she took the blow of a pirate spear into her shoulder. Crying with pain she slumped to the ground.

Gryffyn jumped forward to protect her, he shielded her body with his arms but he had no weapon, so Cutwulf played with him as he gesticulated with the point of his sword.

"Just try me Celt, I have been longing to cut through one of you for some time now." He exclaimed.

Gryffyn raised himself up and said "you have always been a threat to our family Cutwulf but you never quite achieve do you?" And with that he lunged towards a stave which leaned beside a wall nearby, picked it up and turned to face Cutwulf, while he pushed his daughter behind at the same time.

Cutwulf laughed. "Oh this is much better Celt. I do not take much pleasure in killing an unarmed man but now this will be fun. Keep the others in hold while I play with this toy."

This last instruction he directed at his three companions who grabbed Sion and Yeshua and held them both at knife-point.

Cutwulf leaped from his horse and approached Gryffyn with his sword held out.

Gryffyn tried to strike the first blow but Cutwulf sidestepped and nearly cut the stave in half.

Gryffyn backed off and Cutwulf turned to strike himself this time. Gryffyn just managed to parry the blow but his stave was cut once more and half of it dangled from the small piece left in his hand. It was clear that Cutwulf was the better fighter and had the better weapons. This fight would not last long.

Cutwulf laughed. "You might as well give up now Celt and place your neck down for me to cleave, to prevent any further pain or suffering."

However his smile turned to dismay as a small rock appeared out of the sky and struck him on the shoulder.

He cried in alarm and pain, just as another rock ricocheted off his forehead leaving a nasty gouge.

"What in the name of Woden is this?" he cried, as he clutched his bleeding brow.

However, soon more rocks rained down on him and his companions, sending them scurrying quickly away from the alleyway and the barrage of rocks.

Gryffyn looked up to see Joses and others on the roof of one of the buildings as they spread out with slingshots and rocks in their hands, ready to send down more if the pirates returned.

One of the pirates showed his head around the corner but quickly retreated under a hail of rocks.

Gryffyn called up to the next level. "Thank you my friends. I don't know what would have happened without you."

Joses called down, "they interrupted my wedding and struck my mother. That is a crime unpardonable in my mind."

Yeshua, who was tending his mother, then said, "quickly, we must all get away before they return once more." He waved up towards his brother and led the group through a gateway into another courtyard.

They were all pleased to see that Yeshua's mother was okay.

Yeshua turned to his three companions and said, "you must go now I think."

Gryffyn stepped forward. "Thank you Yeshua, we needed to get away quickly, you are our saviour."

Sion rolled his eyes slightly but if Yeshua noticed anything he didn't remark on it.

"You are welcome, I think that man knew you, am I right?"

Gryffyn. "Yes he has a bit of a vendetta against my family. I believe you and your family will be safe once more when we are gone. We are sorry to have disrupted your brother's wedding and got your mother injured. I hope you can forgive us?"

Sion rolled his eyes again. This time Yeshua looked at him before replying.

"I think you are strange people, from a strange place but I wish you well and may Yahweh protect you in your journey. Sion, I am sorry we did not have that conversation, perhaps another day."

He shook their hands as they made their way out of the far side of the courtyard, they smiled at Yeshua's mother as they went.

Gryffyn turned to his companions. "Sion, do you know the way back?"

The monk nodded. "Yes, Gryffyn, it is actually not very far."

"Good we have to get there soon, before Cutwulf knows where we are."

They sped along alleyways and didn't encounter anyone before they reached a building that looked like many others .

Sion led them inside and there was The Book where they left it.

He quickly opened it, they held hands and when Sion touched The Book, all three disappeared.

Later Gryffyn sat alone with Sion.

"I can't risk putting my daughter in danger Sion, Cutwulf and...others are getting too dangerous."

Sion looked unhappy but nodded. "I agree my Lord. If you protect the outside of The Book, I will see what I can do to protect the inside."

Gryffyn smiled briefly. "I hope this is not farewell Sion and that we will enjoy more episodes together. I will explain to my daughter, she will be sad to miss you."

Sion also smiled. "She is a special one Gryffyn, I know I will see her again soon."

CHAPTER TWENTY TWO

Was Briana scared off from The Book following the stories about Cutwulf?

Of course not.

The Book was just too thrilling and the opportunities it threw up were just too good to miss out on.

The Book had been a revelation to her and what was best, was that it was giving her confidence in the real world. While many of her friends descended into worlds created by cgi, she was living out her stories in person and having an amazing time.

The knowledge of this and the fact that she was part of something that had been going on for centuries, stirred her young mind and gave her greater confidence about dealing with the real world. Nothing seemed too much trouble any more and many of things which had seemed important before paled into insignificance.

Who cared if someone died in a soap opera when you could relive the Battle of Bosworth Field?

What did it matter if PK (a superstar rapper) appeared on a TV show or not, when you could watch a black hole form?

What did it matter if someone called her a nasty name at school, compared with the horrors the soldiers went through in the

Napoleonic Wars?

This last visit was in response to a school project but Briana had no real way of articulating the real horrors she saw, heard and felt.

Sometimes the real world did intrude on her happiness from time to time and one day she came home from an English lesson, full of perturbation and Ysabel asked what the problem was.

"Bloody Shakespeare." Briana grumbled.

"Briana, what have I told you about your language?"

"Sorry Mum. But he is so boring. Why do we have to study his plays, they are from like five hundred years ago!"

Ysabel was secretly pleased with her daughter's knowledge of the timescales involved, hoping it wasn't a lucky guess. She replied, "because they are supposed to be the best in the English language."

"Do you really think that Mum?" Briana enquired

Ysabel managed to barely pause before she said "of course I do Briana. When you get older you'll come to appreciate them more. Why don't we see what Sion can do?"

"Oh no, I don't want more Shakespeare!" Briana exclaimed

"Let's see what Sion says first and take it from there" Ysabel said in a conciliatory fashion. So upstairs they trooped and Ysabel asked Sion for his help

"Hello Sion. Briana thinks that Shakespeare is boring. Is there anything you can show us which might change her mind?"

Sion smiled. "Well, we could go and see one of his plays being performed by the man himself."

Quite soon the three of them were standing in one of the smelliest places that Briana had ever visited. Whereas the smell in India had been intense but somehwat pleasing, here it was just rank. They stood in a street outside a run down looking building.

The street itself was a combination of mud and stones and the buildings were mainly made of wood in quite a rough fashion. Street hawkers were peddling their wares and there seemed to be quite a few ladies, who were obviously peddling themselves.

Sion spoke as Ysabel directed her daughter's gaze from the ladies to the pedlars. "We are in London in the early Autumn of 1593, outside the theatre known as Newington Butts..." He indicated towards the run down building before continuing, "...a plague has been raging for the last year..." catching Ysabel's horrified look he pacified her by saying, "...don't worry I have made precautions to make sure we are safe."

Ysabel still looked concerned but slightly less so.

So Sion continued his tale. "Because of the plague, the theatres have been closed for many months." Briana looked at him questioningly, so Sion explained. "People don't like the ideas of big groups of people in close proximity during times of plague, so the authorities closed the theatres down."

"However, the plague has abated for a while and so the theatre is open once more and we are about to see the premiere of one of Shakespeare's early plays called "The Comedy of Errors."

Briana grumbled to herself, "oh great."

Sion didn't hear her or chose to ignore the words and led them forwards into the theatre. A few coins changed hands and they entered.

The first thing that hit Briana were the new smells. Some foul, some sweet, some heady. Everywhere around her were people selling foodstuffs. What the foods were she couldn't tell but the customers were paying and either eating ravenously or stuffing the wares into their clothes.

They passed through the vaulted corridors and into the theatre proper. The theatre was packed. The people had been starved of entertainment during the plague and although they didn't know it, this was just a brief respite before the plague hit again and the theatres would be closed for another year.

Today however, everyone was looking forward to the pleasantries. Well, it looked like they were to Briana, everyone seemed in good spirits and many held flagons of drink and chewed on the various foodstuffs they had purchased or brought with them.

The three newcomers were in the stalls with the majority of the theatre patrons, above them some of the wealthier patrons were in the standing areas in the circle.

Most of the patrons wore simple clothes of plain colours but here and there were more coloured cloths. One man walking towards them stood out, as he was dressed all in black and he headed straight for Sion to whom he nodded.

"Good day Sir, may I ask what order you belong to?" he asked amiably.

Sion looked taken aback, stared for some time at the man but then smiled and replied "I belong to a simple order of Celtic monks not aligned to Rome and not in competition with the destiny of our beloved Queen."

There was obviously something he was keeping to himself because of the knowing look he had in his eye. He also seemed to know the right things to say in this time and place for the man nodded once more and continued "ah, I did look to join an order myself at one point when at Corpus Christi but the time was not right and I felt I still had much to give in the every day world away from the spiritual."

Sion, this time looked a bit bemused before asking "and what is it that you do sir?"

Another man, who was walking by, overheard this question, stopped and said "do? Why this man is the greatest playwright our country has known. Do you not know Christopher Marlowe when you see him sir?"

Sion's eyes widened and said "forgive me good sirs, I am recently travelled to the city with my Lady Ysabel and her daughter…" he indicated towards towards Ysabel and Briana, both men nodded towards them "…we have come from Devonshire and know little of London and her playwrights but thought we would like to see a play today."

Christopher Marlowe smiled and said "then you have chosen well good sir, for this man…" he indicated towards the other man before continuing "…has the potential to be a great playwright and possibly out-write us all."

The second man shook his head and said "ah. You jest sir, I cannot begin to stand even up to your shoulders in magnificence. I look merely to delight the crowds with my simple diversions."

Marlowe then said "well, we shall see how your new play goes today sir and will report back to you most verily." The other man nodded and walked away.

Realisation began to dawn on Briana who said quietly "was that Will Shakespeare?"

Marlowe did not hear her but Sion replied, "yes, you are in the presence of the greatest playwright in the country…" he indicated towards Marlowe "…and the man who is to succeed him and become the best known writer in the English speaking world." He indicated towards the departing Shakespeare who had made his way towards the stage.

Marlowe had turned his attention to Ysabel. "My good Lady the stalls are too base for a gentle beauty such as you, will you not have me find you and your daughter a place in the circle which more befits a lady of your grace?"

Ysabel turned quickly to Sion and Briana and said, "ooh I like him!" Before turning back to Marlowe once more "Nay good Sir. I will join the people in the stalls, so to enjoy the play as they do."

Marlowe nodded his acceptance and taking her arm said "then let me lead you to a spot I know, where you get the acoustics and splendour of the performance at its most bountiful."

And off he led Ysabel, with Sion and Briana trailing along behind, feeling slightly left out.

Briana felt the spot to which Marlowe led them, was much the same as any other spot in the hall but didn't say anything.

In the place where they were now stood, they were surrounded by the masses who seemed to be carrying on with every day life while waiting; eating, drinking, chatting and doing business. One man was even receiving a hair cut.

The play started and Briana actually enjoyed it much more than she expected to. A lot of it was simple comedy made up of the fact that two sets of two men looked the same and seemed to keep on getting mixed up with each other. Each pair was played by the same man on stage, which did make it confusing at times and also left the poor men running around wildly. Some of the jokes went straight over Briana's head but the crowd seemed to find them funny. The visual comedy though was easy to follow and often hilarious.

The crowd often joined in with the proceedings by shouting, throwing things and one lady even bared her breasts briefly during one apparently lewd joke. This set everyone except for Ysabel and Sion laughing. Briana couldn't help but smile.

After a while there came a break and the work of the day started up once more, if it had ever ceased in the first place. The barber had a new customer, the food retailers were once more in sight and the lady who had bared her breasts seemed to be heading upstairs with another gentleman.

Marlowe got them all a jug of wine, he somehow managed to procure some wooden goblets from somewhere and started to share it around. He passed one to Briana who tried not to look at her mother but Ysabel merely raised her eyebrows in resignation and took one herself.

Briana was thoroughly enjoying herself, the smell had seemed to die down or at least she had got used to it. The play was better than expected and now she was getting to drink some wine too. It tasted slightly sweet but she was enjoying it.

Marlowe was still talking to Ysabel who seemed to be enjoying the conversation.

Sion had wanted to talk to Marlowe himself for some reason but the playwright said he would join him later. Therefore the monk excused himself and headed off towards the toilets, which apparently were just a window opening out on to a gutter. After he had been gone a few minutes, a sudden commotion occurred over to their left.

People were moving hurriedly out of the way of someone or something. After a while Briana heard a man calling out "make way, make way for the Queen!"

The crowd parted before him and behind him in came Queen Elizabeth, looking very regal. She was tall with long, flowing red hair. The crowd bowed in a ripple before her and her entourage.

She seemed to be heading towards the stage when suddenly she spotted someone to her side. "You!" she cried. Everyone turned to look at the object of her exclamation.

Ysabel and Briana followed her gaze as the audience parted once more to reveal a shocked looking Sion.

The Queen turned to her men and called out. "Seize the Papist for he has done me and the people of England much wrongs."

Sion didn't wait to be captured but turned and headed out through the crowd, who weren't quite sure what to do. The armed men headed after him, the Queen started to do the same but one of her men said "nay, my Lady you should stay here, we will track down the Jesuit."

The Queen looked like she was going to argue but then nodded and stayed where she was while some of her men set off in pursuit of Sion.

Marlowe turned back towards Ysabel and asked "why should the Queen be after your friend?"

Ysabel looked genuinely surprised by the turn of events and a bit shocked, so therefore she replied, "I have no idea but I can vouchsafe for him, he is no papist."

Marlowe decided to believe her.

"She thinks he has done her some wrong in the past but that doesn't worry me completely, as I myself have had some run ins with her majesty and her council, so would not be averse to helping one who had similarly vexed or been persecuted by her. Come quickly, I know of an alternative way through to the passageway to which they are heading."

He headed off towards the stage so that Ysabel and Briana had to move quickly in pursuit. He led them on to the stage itself and then through a curtain out the back. This was obviously where the actors hung out and they were surprised to be interrupted by Marlowe, a lady and a girl.

One man stood up and addressed the fast moving Marlowe.

"Where are you going Christopher?"

The big man stopped briefly to address his questionner "on an errand of mercy Will, please don't delay us."

Shakespeare retorted, "then I must perchance come with thee and join this errand."

Marlowe sighed. "You must not Will, for we go against the will of the Queen and you must not risk your good name with her."

"Good name? That Lady does not even know my name. Whereas this good Lady..." he indicated towards Ysabel
"... is a damsel in distress, who needs our help. So let us not tarry and make haste."

With that both Shakespeare and Marlowe headed off once more at such a pace that Ysabel and Briana struggled to follow.

Soon they found themselves at the back of the theatre in an alleyway, which led them back to the main street. It was obvious which way Sion and the men at arms had headed, as there was disarray ahead and people were looking down the street.

The quartet ran quickly and soon reached a tavern which stood at the end of the street.

Entering, they spied a scene of terror for Briana and Ysabel. For there stood Sion facing three men at arms, two with swords drawn, the third pointing a musket at the monk.

One of the men called out, "don't move priest or we will send you back to Rome in a box."

Sion trembled as he said "I'm not from Rome, I'm from Devon."

The men sneered but Sion continued, "my allegiance is with Christ not the Bishop in Rome."

The men laughed and the one with the musket shouted, "don't play with us priest, the Queen wants you and we will bring you back to her, alive or with eyes which look no more."

While this interplay had been going on, Shakespeare and Marlowe had been making their way through the tavern and were now close to the scene.

Shakespeare addressed the men at arms. "Good sirs, the priest speaks the truth. He has merely escorted this fine lady..." he indicated towards Ysabel before he continued "...up from the West Country and has no desire to cause problems with any man, let alone the Queen. That magisterial lady must be mistaken, for this man of the cloth has never been to London before."

The men at arms listened to this pretty speech but it seemed to have little or no effect on them, for one of the knife men said, "enough, we will take this priest with us to the Queen forthwith."

To which Marlowe replied, "you will not sir." With that he moved towards them.

The knife man said "I will sir."

This time Shakespeare interjected, "you will not sir."

The knife man was more forceful this time. "I WILL sir." Then he moved once more towards Sion. Shakespeare moved across but the man with the musket barred his path and they started to tussle.

The two men with knives went straight at Sion but Marlowe jumped into their way and started to fight with both of them together.

Everything then happened at once, first the musket went off, taking out a large part of the ceiling but seemingly not injuring anyone, a woman screamed and one of the knife-men turned, as did Marlowe who suddenly cried out himself, as first one and then another knife took him in the chest and neck.

The men at arms all looked at each other. They were all now unarmed and had stabbed the wrong man, plus the rest of the tavern were not looking on at them with good favour. They decided to beat a hasty retreat.

Will, Ysabel, Briana and Sion all ran over to Marlowe. Sion and Shakespeare each held him and Shakespeare cradled his head in his lap.

Blood was coming from Marlowe's mouth but he managed to speak. "Is this a dagger which I see before me or the instrument of death?"

Shakespeare smiled at his ailing friend and said "I like that one, perchance I could steal it?"

Marlowe nodded. "You may, I was to use it in my next play but I can't see that happening now."

The others started to voice their disagreement but suddenly he started choking and convulsing and more blood issued forth. Briefly it stopped and he said quietly "and now it ends. The rest is silence." The light went from his eyes and his head dropped.

Shakespeare howled before gathering himself and holding his friend's head he said gently "good night sweet Prince and may flights of angels sing thee to thy rest."

Then gently he lay Marlowe's head down.

He looked at the others. "That was something I have been working on but I think my good friend Christopher deserved something even better."

Sion shook his head. "His life ended with glory and I think your words were a fitting epitaph."

He looked at Ysabel and Briana quickly before continuing, "And now you must forgive us but the Queen is probably still after me. My travails have already caused this good man's death, I would not want you or anyone else to suffer needlessly in my place again. So I would suggest that we make haste and depart this city before we cause even more sorrows, therefore you should leave this tavern quickly."

Shakespeare nodded his head and shook Sion's hand. He did the same with Briana before turning to Ysabel. "My lady, London will be bereft at thy parting and a small piece of my heart will go with thee. If you ever return, look up Will Shakespeare and I will write a sonnet to thy name."

He took her hand and kissed it gently, before taking his leave.

Sion turned to Ysabel and Briana and said, "help me with the body".

He indicated towards the recumbent form of Marlowe.

If Ysabel and Briana were confused by this request, they said nothing and helped Sion pick up the dead man.

They made their way carefully back through the streets, not talking about what had just happened.

They managed to get back to The Book without any further problems. Laying the body of Marlowe down in the blackness inside The Book, all three touched the pages and were taken back to the 21st century.

Ysabel asked the question that both she and Briana had been dying to ask.

"Sion. Why was Queen Elizabeth after your blood?"

Sion looked surprised at the question and replied, "my Lady. That was not really Queen Elizabeth. That was Morwenna. The member of your family who killed her own Father and dwells within The Book. She recognised me at once of course but fortunately as I was not with you, she did not realise that you and Briana were there, or else it could have been disastrous."

Ysabel looked shocked. "Morwenna. I didn't realise."

Briana said, "Mum, who is Morwenna?"

Ysabel replied. "She is one of the ones I mentioned to you. The ones like Cutwulf who are in The Book and we need to be wary of. Normally Sion can protect us but sometimes they put all their powers into the story to turn it to their side and that means that we can be vulnerable. Isn't that right Sion?"

"Yes my Lady. As soon as I saw Morwenna, I knew she had control over the story and I had to lead her away from you two. I never dreamt that you would follow us and not only that, but come with Marlowe and Shakespeare."

Ysabel replied. "But if we hadn't, you would probably not be here talking to us now. So let us be grateful for the interjection of Mr Shakespeare and Mr Marlowe."

At the mention of the names Briana sighed. "Poor Christopher, I liked him. What a shame he had to die."

Sion nodded but said "he was due to be stabbed later that very same day anyway in an argument over a bill. However many think that he was embroiled in espionage and had been working for Walsingham, the Queen's spymaster. Perhaps what happened today was closer to the truth than what is normally reported."

He concluded, "I liked Marlowe but his death left a gap which Shakespeare filled and that led him to becoming the finest playwright the world has ever known. Whether he borrowed some ideas from Marlowe we shall never know." He winked at them both and departed.

Back inside The Book, Sion bent over the recumbent body of Christopher Marlowe, with a tear in his eye and said, "Christos, my old friend what were you doing in there?"

He nearly screamed when the body opened its eyes...

CHAPTER TWENTY THREE

Other trips followed but Ysabel decided that they should lessen the number as Briana approached her end of year exams.

Briana however, was having the time of her young life and couldn't wait for the next adventure.

The only problem was that she couldn't tell anyone about it and sometimes the knowledge she gained was not able to be used, which could make it difficult in classes or just in general conversation.

A prime example was one day when she came home from school excited by a lesson about human evolution. They had watched a fabulous programme about early human ancestors and relatives, and the fact that some of them had been found just down the road at Kent's Cavern near Torquay made it even more interesting.

Enthused by this, her mum suggested that they pay a visit to The Book and see what Sion could come up with.

On entering The Book the monk had a few ideas but said, "of course it would be good to see some of the earliest Devon inhabitants, wouldn't it?"

Ysabel and Sion, slightly unsure about what he meant just nodded their assent.

Their surroundings blurred and they found themselves standing on a grassy hillside, overlooking a large grassy plain.

They stood looking at the tranquil view and could spot quite a few animals moving over the plain. Not wanting to break the tranquility, Sion spoke softly.

"Before I show you what we are here to see, I need to tell you a little bit about where we are."

He indicated the hillside on which we they were standing.

"We are approximately one million years in the past and..." Briana let out a little gasp of surprise but Sion continued, "...where we are standing is pretty much the coast of modern day South Devon. It will change over time due to weathering and coastal erosion but behind us..." he indicated over his shoulder "...will be Newton Abbot, over to our left Teignmouth and Dawlish. And that way..." he pointed to their right "...will be Torbay. The plain in front of us will all be under the English Channel."

"We are currently in a slightly warmer spell, with temperatures similar to modern day Mediterranean countries but at other times it will be more like modern day Scandinavia with mild summers but very cold winters."

"The fauna is very different to today. We've got a great view of a small herd of aurochs over there." He pointed towards a group of about twenty large cattle-like animals on the plain. "And over there..." this time he indicated towards their left on the plain "...is a group of Mammoths. We can't see any at the moment but you might also see woolly rhinoceros. Hunting these large animals you might have hyenas as large as lions or cave bears or even polar bears coming down from the ice and tundra to the North."

"But what we have really come to see is a group down on the

plain." He indicated towards a a wooded glade a mere couple of hundred yards away from where they stood.

There was a path of sorts leading down that way, what made the path they weren't sure and after the talk of hyenas, lions and cave bears, Briana was a bit worried about what they might find.

It actually was quite idyllic, it felt like a mild late spring day back home and the air was clear, there were birds chattering and the sounds from the mammoths and the aurochs from the plain resonated clearly across the whole area.

Presently, they reached the little wooded glade. The trees were much as they would see back home and even Briana's untutored eye could spot oak, beech and sycamore. She even spotted a couple of blackbirds chattering away on an oak branch, what could be more British than that? Obviously a million years was little time to many of these species, who had been around for many hundreds of millennia and sometimes even millions of years.

But then you had the mammoths, hyenas and aurochs. You couldn't imagine walking around South Devon in the modern day, and seeing those wandering free.

Sion, who must have somehow been aware of what Briana was thinking spoke carefully. "It is a shame to see these species come and go, our world is lessened by the loss of them. However many other species have lived and died before and many more will do the same before the end of time. One of the most interesting species, we are just about to see."

Briana wondered what kind of species they were going to see next. All the talk of Hyenas and Cave Lions, made her wonder whether they would come across a really scary monster. When did the dinosaurs live? Surely that was long before now?

Sion led them into the wooded glade on the plain. A small stream meandered through short, stunted trees, while birds chirruped away, obviously concerned about the new arrivals. After a few minutes, Sion held up his hand to halt them and put his other hand to his mouth to make sure they knew to keep quiet. He needn't have worried, both Ysabel and Briana had been walking along in complete silence.

After a moment he motioned towards a small group, through the trees. There were about fifteen in total, of varying ages and they were located around a small group of rocks which sat next to the winding stream.

Briana stared in wonder. They were people but not people, if that made any sense. Both the males and females had a light covering of auburn hair but it was sparse enough in places to tell they were olive skinned. It was difficult to tell exactly but it appeared that they were slightly shorter than modern humans.

They walked erect but with a slight swinging motion in their arms and hips.

It was in their faces however that the visitors found their keenest interest. The dark eyes were set below a small forehead and deep brow. Their jaws looked much stronger than modern humans and their teeth also looked slightly more robust, as if they had to tackle hardier foodstuffs than their later counterparts.

Briana noticed a few of them wore cloaks made of animal hide but there seemed no obvious distinction between who wore one and who did not.

Both Ysabel and Briana looked at Sion questioningly. So he spoke softly to themselves

"What you are looking at are some of the first hominid s to inhabit Britain. This species is a precursor to our own species, Homo Sapiens and is sometimes called Homo Antecessor or sometimes Homo Erectus but being honest it was an ever changing species, so the titles mean little. Some will head back south during a particularly cold spell and mix once more with other hominid species and be part of the species we now call Neanderthals. What became of the ones that stayed, no-one really knows."

"They mainly live in small family units like this one but from time to time, one of the larger females will head off with the young males or females and swap them with other local groups. In what will become South Devon, there are perhaps fifteen or twenty groups just like this one and somehow they all know that a change in the gene pool is good for the sustained health and well being of each group."

"Their society is matriarchal, that is run by the older females and that one..." he indicated towards a large, uncloaked female sitting with her back to a rock "...is the dominant female in the group."

"The females maintain their homes and families..." again he indicated towards the group and this time Briana noticed the animal hides which seemed to be tethered to the trees to create a quite sophisticated shelter "...while the males are responsible for sourcing the food, which consists of anything they can get their hands on. From shellfish and small animals to carrion and nuts and berries."

He waved towards the plain. "They don't often bring down a mammoth or an auroch but they will sometimes scare off a group of lions or hyenas who have managed to make a kill. They won't stay long, they will use their stone axes to cut off some meat before the beasts get brave once more and return to their kill."

"They haven't learned how to make fire yet, so most of their food is raw. However they will sometimes source fire from natural sources and use it to bring more flavour and a different consistency to their food. Sometimes they are able to keep the fire going for some time but then the heavy rains will come and wash away everything. So then they wait once more."

"Would you like to get closer and meet them?"

Briana looked in concern at Sion and Ysabel. With a slight quaver in her voice she asked, "will it be safe, will they not see us as competition?"

Sion shook his head. "No, for some reason this species at this time is much more welcoming than its near relatives such as ourselves or chimpanzees. We should be safe but don't make any abrupt gestures or sounds."

Without waiting to discuss it more, he started walking gently down towards the group. Ysabel and Briana felt compelled to follow.

The group looked up in alarm as they approached but Sion walked forward with palms held down to indicate that he intended no aggression and that seemed to pacify the group who just watched the approaching humans with interest. Ysabel and Briana followed suit and together all three walked up to the dominant female.

Sion delved into his monk's cloak and brought out two items and said, "I took the liberty of bringing a couple of gifts to share."

He unwrapped cloth around one item and revealed a large wholemeal loaf, the other cloth revealed a bottle of cloudy liquid.

He unstoppered the bottle, took a swig and licked his lips with relish before handing it to the female saying,

"Apple juice from the friary in 1473." Whether he said this for the benefit of the female hominid or for his human friends was unclear.

The female sniffed the bottle and then mimicked Sion drinking from the bottle. The rest of the group watched alertly. She finished and gave what can only be described as a smile and made some sounds which set off the rest of the group who responded in earnest. Whether they were talking with words or just indicating their feeling through vocal noises, it was not clear but you could tell that she liked it and this made everyone happy.

Sion then tore a chunk off of the bread and handed the chunk and rest of the loaf to the female. Again she sniffed before taking a bite of the bread. On this occasion she took her time and chewed, before letting out a grunt of pleasure. Once again the rest of the group joined the happy chorus.

Sion took two more bottles and loaves from his cloak and passed them to the female who took another bite and swig before passing to the lesser females surrounding her. The group passed the profferings around while chattering with pleasure in their guttural dialect.

The lead female, then made noises at one of her females who brought forth an animal hide and unwrapped it. Inside was a range of items including nuts, fruits and what looked like strips of leather.

Sion turned to Ysabel and Briana. "Eat some of the nuts and fruit for otherwise they will be offended, however do not touch the strips as they are dried meat. I will have one of those as I am not vegetarian like you two."

They did as he said and soon the group were all partaking of the shared repast and chattering away to each other, even though neither side knew what the other was saying.

A couple of the hominids went to the stream with carved out wooden bowls and offered the water to their human guests. Briana, who would rarely drink plain water back home, drank some and was delighted at the purity of the taste. She wasn't sure if it really did taste better than the water at home or her mind believed it did because of the idyllic surroundings of an Eden-like prehistoric Earth.

One of the hominid females started taking an interest in her clothing. At first she thought she was just interested in the strange fabric of her t-shirt and jeans but it soon became clear that she wanted to see what was underneath the outer clothing.

Ysabel started to look concerned and came over towards Briana.

The hominid female made some noises toward the dominant female, who turned to two others and gave obvious instructions.

Two younger hominids were brought forward, one female and one male.

The dominant female led the younger female and held her out in offering to Ysabel. At the same time the second female led Briana towards the young male hominid and placed them standing towards each other. She made some sounds as she did this.

Ysabel looked to and fro in consternation and Briana appeared absolutely terrified about what was going to happen next.

Ysabel looked at Sion, who suddenly had realisation in his eyes. "Ah. I hadn't considered this. They would like to swap Briana for this young female here, so that Briana can mate with the young male and keep their gene pool fresh." He indicated towards the different individuals as he said this.

"Oh god they can't do that with Briana" Ysabel cried.

"Mum!" Briana called distraught.

Ysabel started to head towards Briana but the dominant female barred her way.

Although she was no shrinking violet, Ysabel did not relish the idea of having to force her way past the female and attempt to recover Briana, especially as more of the hominids, include the males were now getting to their feet, obviously disturbed by the panic in Ysabel and Briana's voices.

More softly Ysabel said, "oh god Sion what are we going to do?" Before turning once more to Briana and saying, "just stay calm Briana, we will sort this out."

Sion looked on in consternation but also spoke calmly and softly. "I honestly don't know Ysabel. I hadn't even thought about anything like this happening. They seem friendly enough but I wouldn't like to think what will happen if we try and take Briana away."

They both looked towards the group of hominids who had now surrounded Briana and the young male. Briana was shaking as she called out once more "M-um!"

Ysabel made a strong effort to stay calm and said, "don't worry Briana, Sion has sorted out more difficult situations than this in the past." Even if she didn't believe it herself, she tried to make sure that her daughter was not going to get even more stressed.

Sion was muttering to himself. "There is no way of extracting the girl from under their noses, there are just too many of them. I can't think of any way of distracting them."

Ysabel interjected. "Could we wait until tonight and try and get her away when they all asleep?"

Sion shook his head. "Unfortunately no, they never all go to sleep together. They always leave one or two on guard in case of attack."

Ysabel looked sullen and Sion still stared at, the now surrounded, Briana in consternation. Suddenly his eyes lit up. "Ysabel, you were on the right tracks. I have an idea."

Once again he delved into his, apparently bottomless, pockets in his cloak and drew forth some more bottles. This time Ysabel had an idea it wasn't apple juice.

"Apple brandy" said Sion. "Hand made by monks for centuries." He unstoppered a bottle and took a sniff. "Mmmm" he exclaimed

The hominids took a new interest in this new reaction from the monk and one or two took an involuntary step forward.

Sion unstoppered the rest of the bottles and passed a couple to Ysabel before offering the first bottle to the dominant female. He called gently to Ysabel and Briana. "Drink sparingly for this is strong stuff and we want to make sure they drink as much as they need."

The dominant female was already sniffing the bottle and suddenly coughed in surprise at the smell. She did not look so positive as she sipped from the bottle. She looked at first in surprise, then distaste, then a big smile passed across her face as the liquid sank down her throat and she rubbed her chest with pleasure.

The other bottles started to get passed around from lips to lips and the hominids drank greedily. The three humans also showed willing, joining in the drinking but their apparent supping was masked as they actually closed their mouths and only tasted the minimal amount of brandy.

The sounds from the group evolved and soon something akin to singing could be heard from them all. Ysabel could discern little difference between this group and their actions and those of a drunken group on a Saturday night in Newton Abbot.

Maybe the only difference was the fact that all of this group seemed very happy. This was partly aided by the fact that Sion seemed to have an endless supply of the brandy, Ysabel hesitated to think what would have happened if he were to run out.

Some of the younger and older hominids were already getting drowsy, so much so that a few were nodding off to sleep.

One of the females (the one who had taken Briana), seemed to decide that Ysabel was a sister to her (perhaps because they had swapped daughters) and put her arm around Ysabel and started making sounds which sounded to Ysabel almost like an old sea shanty. Ysabel joined in with the lilting tones in order to show willing.

Soon the party got quieter and quieter as the hominids seemed to succumb to the gentle intoxication of the brandy, until only a few remained awake. One was the dominant female and Sion took it upon himself to sit next to her and share a bottle, as Ysabel edged closer to Briana who feigned tiredness herself and had laid down on the ground.

One of the last two remaining males fell down asleep and his friend who went to look at him, took one more swig and laid down to sleep himself.

Now all that remained was the dominant female who was happily chirruping away to Sion as they leaned side by side. Sion motioned to Ysabel to go to Briana, so she did so.

Finally the female succumbed. She gave a large burp before lying down on the soft grass.

After a little moment of stillness, Sion indicated for them all to stand up slowly which they did.

Then he motioned for Ysabel and Briana to walk over to the tree towards the exit to the little glade, where they had spent the last hour or so.

A couple of the hominids stirred slightly as Briana and Ysabel walked through them. Each time this occurred the pair stopped to make sure that they did not fully wake up.

Finally there was just the pair of large males to pass to reach Sion and safety but just as they reached the pair, one of them started to turn. He raised his arms and gave a large yawn. Ysabel and Briana looked at each other in panic, both wondering whether they should make a run for it but then the large male rolled over once more and was soon snoring away loudly.

Sion beckoned them over and the three quickly made their escape from the glade.

Not until they were halfway up the hill did any of them look around or speak.

Sion said in a concerned voice. "My Lady. I had no idea that there could be any danger to us and particularly to you or Mistress Briana."

Ysabel replied, "Sion, there was no way you could have anticipated that happening and I think your solution was inspired. They will all be alright won't they?"

Sion nodded. "Oh yes, they will have a bit of a headache tomorrow but otherwise no worse for the experience."

Ysabel smiled. "Good. I would hate to think that we had harmed them at all. They were a lovely group, even if they did want to take my daughter!"

Sion nodded agreement and said, "I would not be surprised if some had been intoxicated before. Sometimes fruits and saps can become fermented in the wild and there is evidence of chimpanzees enjoying the alcoholic results. I would be surprised if our hominid relatives did not do the same thing."

Ysabel turned to her daughter as they reached the crest of the hill. "Are you okay Briana?"

The girl nodded but looked visibly shaken.

"We will get you home and get you a nice bath and cup of tea, that always cures everything I have found." She said with a little hint of sarcasm, but not much, in her voice.

As the three headed back to their starting point, Ysabel turned to look back to look out at the plain beneath them and said, "it is a veritable Garden of Eden out there. It is such a shame to think how we will destroy it over time."

She called down on to the plain towards the slow moving mammoths and aurochs and towards the unseen hominids, cave lions and hyenas. "Enjoy it while you can folks. Man is coming along to muck it all up!"

And with that she turned back and the three of them left that world to return to their own once more.

Briana thought. "How would I explain any of that in my human evolution lessons?"

CHAPTER TWENTY FOUR

Ysabel was beginning to wonder about the effect The Book was having on her. Just like Briana, she had been introduced to it at a young age and had been fascinated. But then teenage life seemed to get in the way and therefore hair, boys, Duran Duran and clothes became more important than reliving the past – which seemed to be what she had begun to associate The Book with.

She kept The Book after her father died but didn't spend much time in it because the time never seemed right. Her husband knew very little about what it was, it just loitered in the loft along with other family heirlooms and there always seemed to be something else to do with him and then when Briana came along, their lives changed anyway.

Then after Derek died, she found that the role of mother, father and breadwinner took up all of her time and she began to forget about The Book.

Now that she and Briana were using it again, she wished she had spent more time in it earlier in her life and had enjoyed more time in there with Derek. Well it was too late for that now and she looked forward to enjoying it more.

However, tonight was a girl's night out. She hadn't been out in ages and was looking forward to putting her gladrags on, getting a bit pie-eyed and just having a bit of fun.

Briana was waiting in the hall when she came down ready to go out.

"Now don't stay up too late."

"Can I go in The Book?" Her daughter asked, trying to look as cherubic as it was possible for a teenage girl to look.

"Don't pull that look on me young lady." She replied but thinking about it, she would probably be safer in there with Sion than watching TV or causing trouble in the house all alone.

"Only if you stay with Sion and get to bed before 9:30." It was just after 6pm now.

"Yes Mum, of course."

Briana kissed her on the cheek, and marvelled at the fact she could see her Mum had her legs out as Ysabel opened the door and headed out into the cool early evening air.

Briana quickly went upstairs and entered her bedroom. The room was much tidier than it had been in the past and The Book held pride of place on a new bookshelf. Briana went straight to the shelf and took down The Book.

She pondered what to do, did she have a plan of what to see or ask for tonight or should she just wing it?

She decided to open The Book at random and see where it took her. She placed The Book on her bed, placed her fingers on the side and opened The Book at about three quarters of the way through. The pages alighted on just two articles, the first, entitled "Reptilian Monsters", only took up a little bit of the two page spread and did not even attract Briana's attention. However the larger article on "Republic of Rome" caught her eye straight away. The words "intrigue", "murder", "deception", "war" and "tyranny" seemed to jump out from the pages and grab her attention.

So it was only natural that she place her hand on the open book on the relevant article and the now-familiar sensation took her into another world.

Sion was already waiting for her when she re-appeared into darkness. She was slightly disappointed after reading so much about excitement to be in another dark place.

"Welcome Mistress Briana, you are on your own tonight?"

This was obvious but Briana still replied, "yes, Mum is on a girl's night out."

Sion nodded sagely as if he really understood what a "Girl's night out" in the 21st century entailed. He continued.

"You have chosen the Republic of Rome, is it for a school project? Do you have a particular time or event in mind?"

Briana shook her head. "No it was just a lucky dip, I opened The Book and there it was."

Sion nodded. "Ah, a fortuitous chance then. This is a fabulous period in history and one that the original masters of The Book were very interested in, as they looked up to Rome as the pinnacle of human achievement."

He smiled. "There are many great events and people I could show you. Such as the great Hannibal taking his elephants over the alps, or Tiberius Gracchus leading the plebs against the senate or Scipio Africanus finally defeating the Carthaginians. What type of event would you like to see?"

Briana mumbled that she was not sure but the words that had jumped out from the page revisited her brain and somehow Sion seemed to know what she was thinking.

"Ah, you want intrigue and back stabbing. There are a few periods which would work but I think I know the best time for us."

CHAPTER
TWENTY FIVE

The blackness disappeared and they both, Briana and Sion, were startled by the brightness of the light. They were in a small street in a built up town, the walls were grubby and the streets were a mixture of cobble, grit and sand. There was a slight stench but the water that ran along the street was remarkably clean.

There was no one to be seen as yet.

"This is Rome itself, in what we now know as 88BC, of course the people living here don't know that in 88 years or so a chap by the name of Jesus is going to be born in far off Judea, so of course they give the year a different name but for our purposes I think we will stick with 88 BC. Ok?" Sion looked questioningly at Briana who just looked perplexed.

"Erm sure."

"The reason we have come to this place and time, is that I would like you to meet two of the people who will change Rome for ever. There is also a possibility that we might even see a third man, who is equally important to the history and end of the republic of Rome but any interaction with him would be more fraught."

"The first man is called Gaius Marius and he is a low-born man who has gone far. He has been consul more times than should be allowed by law, he is the most important man in Rome and he will go a long way towards making Rome great and powerful. But also he will play a part in Rome changing the way it thinks about itself."

Briana just nodded in response.

"The second person I hope to introduce you to, is a boy who is just 11 years old but he will become better known than any other Roman and he will herald a new age and time in Rome's history. He will even give his name to the Emperors who will follow his lead."

"The third person we might see but hopefully not, is a man by the name of Lucius Cornelius Sulla. He was a friend and colleague of Gaius Marius but now they are on opposite sides of a civil war. Sulla will become even more powerful than Marius, will make himself Dictator and pave the way for later consuls to follow his lead and put themselves ahead of the Senate and eventually become Emperors."

They walked along the street to a corner and they found the new street was much wider and busier than the one they had just left. People were making their way to and fro and some others were selling their wares from small carts or sometimes from the doorways of their houses.

A big building with small featureless statues was the centre of most of the activity, with people coming and going all the time and a large number carrying in or out large pots or jugs.

"That is the tavern of Lucius Sextus, a pleb but a very important man in this part of Rome and the one who is going to help us get in to see Marius."

They walked through the street, having to dodge the people who seemed to believe that they had the right to be there more than Sion and Briana. Briana looked down at her and Sion's clothes, which did seem different from those around them. Sion caught her glances and explained.

"We are dressed as Gaulish merchants, which will explain our odd accent when we speak. Gaul is a collection of tribes to the North-West of Rome, largely in modern day France but they are also the relatives of the Britons. As some of the people we meet will have been to Gaul, we will pretend to be from Britannia, as most Romans will barely have heard of Britannia, let alone been there."

Briana looked confused. "But I thought the Romans invaded Britain and built Bath and...other places?"

Sion smiled. "Oh they did but that is not for another 150 years or so in the times of the Emperors. The boy you are going to meet today, will invade Britain in about 45 years time but he didn't stay to conquer."

The early morning sun was warm and Briana was quite pleased to leave it when they entered the tavern. At first she could see nothing as they came from the bright sunlight into the darker tavern but quickly she realised it was not like the pubs she had been in back home.

The tavern was full of people offering to buy and sell everything. Men selling ceramic pots, others selling food, others selling packets, which she couldn't tell what was inside. There were some women who were not wearing very much and one opened her robe to one of the other customers as Sion and Briana walked past. "Teach the girl how to make love?" she said to Sion, who just hurried Briana past the lady in question towards a counter with a large, dark-haired man beside it.

"Lucius Sextus, greetings!" Sion called as he walked up to the man.

The man filled two earthenware cups from the large jug he was holding (Briana would later learn that this was called an amphora) and said, "Sharnus! I have some excellent Falernian wine here that you will like. I would not normally give it to this rabble but you are a man who likes good things. Who is the girl?"

Sion looked from Briana to Sextus who gave him one of the cups. "This is my cousin's daughter Briana, who I am teaching the ways of trade with the peoples of the Mare Nostrum." He passed the cup to Briana saying, "it will be watered down wine but drink it slowly."

Briana took the cup and tried the wine which was nicer than she had expected, it tasted a bit like squash but not as sweet.

Sion asked, "how are things in the city Sextus?"

Sextus watched them drinking for a moment before replying. "You've visited at a bad time."

He looked around at the tavern to make sure he was not being overheard but the business of the day was noisy and no one was interested in the conversations of the three of them.

"Sulla is just outside the city but cannot enter while he still holds his consular Imperium."

He could see that Briana did not understand, so explained.

"To prevent the consuls or proconsuls, who are sent out to govern the provinces, from seizing power like a King, they are prevented from entering the city while they still hold that power. Once they are normal Senators again they are free to go wherever they want to. Sulla holds that Imperium and therefore cannot enter the city."

"Why should he want to?" Sion asked

"Because he and the "Boni" are worried about the power and support of Gaius Marius, who has now been consul more times than anyone should be. They are worried that he wants to make himself King."

Sion interjected and looked directly at Briana. "The Romans got rid of their Kings a few hundred years ago. They are now ruled by the Patricians, people like Lucius Cornelius Sulla but every now and then a new man, like Gaius Marius, comes through to join them in the high ranks of the Senate and the Patricians don't like it!"

Sextus laughed. "You know as much as I do Sharnus, not bad for someone from so far away."

Sextus didn't really know where Britannia was and he would have been amazed by what he saw if he ever did go, because he had never left the confines of the city of Rome.

"Anyway, the Boni need Sulla to sort Marius out but he can't do anything right now. So he has sent his agents into Rome to cause trouble and undermine Marius wherever he can. Marius is fighting fire with fire and everyone is beginning to take sides. So it is a time to worry about who your enemies might be, who knows what and who would like to get you out of the way."

Sextus looked towards Sion. "You will be wanting to get in to see the big man?" Sion nodded, so Sextus continued "Well, I will try but he is very busy right now and might not see us."

He looked around the tavern and located a red faced woman talking to a leather salesman.

"Livia! I'm off to see the big man, tend the bar will you?"

He led them back through the crowded tavern into the bright street beyond.

Briana looked around at the people more intently after the comments of Sextus and Sion, almost expecting there to be assassins at every turn. However the people seemed to be carrying on their days as per normal and she watched to see what normal was.

The butcher had carcasses hanging in the sun, which he would then take down and proceed to chop up into smaller bits.

Then his assistant would take, proffer and sell these pieces to the people coming to purchase their meat.

Another man was selling knives from a stall outside his house, while his assistant sharpened others with a stone. There was a massive variety of knives available behind the knife seller and each potential buyer indicated what they wanted to use their new purchase for by miming the action in front of the knife seller. Most were looking for kitchen or household knives but one man was trying different knives by performing a stabbing action. Briana wondered if this action was in response to the trouble that Sextus and Sion had been discussing or whether a more every day nefarious explanation was the answer. The knife seller sold his wares to everyone, irrespective of what they wanted them for and Briana would never know the answers to her questions.

Next was a man cutting the hair of one man but he stopped part way through to attend to a screaming man who arrived with blood on his face and holding a cloth to his head.

The barber removed a piece of leather from a basket and took some hand clippers to the man's head and gently removed the cloth. When he had cleared a substantial amount of hair from the man's head it displayed a large cut through the scalp. The barber rolled up the leather, gave it to the man to put in his mouth and proceeded to sew up the man's scalp with large stitches. All the time the man bit down on the leather, grimacing and sweating profusely.

When the barber/surgeon had finished he took some fat from a bowl, smeared it on the man's head, who continued to grimace. The barber then took the leather and a handful of coins before turning back to his hair cutting service once more.

Briana turned her attention to the other street traders, while Sion and Sextus engaged in conversation. Briana noticed Sion pass coins to Sextus, who took them nonchalantly.

The street traders started thinning out and the buildings seemed to become more impressive and cleaner. Where they had been a mixture of sand bricks and wood, they started to become cut stone until they became bright, white buildings.

Even Briana could tell they were moving into the richer parts of town. After a short while they came to a gateway where two men stood. They wore little, just little leather skirts and belts running diagonally across their chests and it was clear from their large chest and arm muscles, together with their well defined abdominals, that they were guards and that they were men not to be messed with. They each held a long staff with a curved blade on the top.

Sextus nodded at them both, slipped some coins into the hand of one and they waved the three of them through.

The gateway led almost immediately to a door where two more men stood, they nodded at Sextus and again they were waved through.

They passed through a hallway into a large room which was nearly full of people. At one end sat a man in a large ornate chair, raised slightly on a small dais. Another man was talking and gesturing towards him, while the man in the ornate chair looked on in a slightly bored fashion. The others in the room seemed to be waiting in line to be called forward to discuss their matters.

Sextus and Sion walked straight past some of them, to a shorter man standing slightly to the side holding a scroll. His dress and short beard showed him to be Greek, though Briana was not to know this. Sextus spoke briefly to the Greek who then beckoned them forward towards the man at the centre of everyone's attention.

The Greek man ignored the gesticulating man and spoke directly to the seated man.

The seated man then looked directly towards Sextus, Sion and Briana. His eyes lingered on all of them in turn before he looked back at the gesticulating and pleading man who had not paused.

"Enough Secundus! I will consider your requests with regards to your father and older brother. Aristophanes here..." he indicated towards the Greek man "...will let you know what happens."

He now stood up and Briana looked at him closely for the first time. He was taller than most of the men around him but not a giant. He had lost most of his hair, was clean shaven and his face showed signs of age and also battle scars.

He wore a toga, the only man in the room to do so, the rest were wearing simple tunics.

He addressed the rest of the room. "That is all for now, you can all go home until tomorrow." Then he walked out of another door beckoning to Aristophanes the Greek as he did so.

He was followed by a boy whom Briana had not noticed until this point, the boy had a strong nose and determined look on his face as he walked through the crowd, who parted in the wake of the main man, out of the room.

Aristophanes turned to the three of them and said, "the great man will see you in the atrium, follow me."

CHAPTER TWENTY SIX

Cutwulf was enjoying his latest role. He hadn't known much about the man until he had immersed himself into the story but now he felt he had found a kindred spirit. This was a role which would keep him entertained for some time.

The man was high born but had also lived in the gutter and there he had associated with some of the worst elements in the City. He knew the whores, thieves, assassins and even the lowly actors. Many of them as friends.

He had an aristocratic wife but also seemed happy to debase himself with dockside whores and even indulge in Greek love from time to time, which wasn't really to Cutwulf's liking but nobody was perfect.

He seemed just as happy dealing with the nefarious parts of the community as well as the top echelons and all of them looked towards him as their leader and the one with the power to do what they wanted him to do, or so they thought.

The Indian episode had seemed promising and it had brought the added bonus of a sight of his old enemy Sion, who could not hide the existence of the woman and the girl who must be of the bloodline of Geraint.

Even the thought of them got his blood boiling and he wanted to lure them into more stories, so that he could do something about them. Killing the girl would really make him happy.

Perhaps this latest role would be the one that proved fruitful.

CHAPTER TWENTY SEVEN

Back in the bright sunlight of the atrium, Briana took some time to discern her surroundings. She soon understood that an atrium was a central square in the middle of the house surrounded by walls on four sides.

In the middle was a small pond or pool, again it was square and surrounded by small fruit and olive trees. It reminded Briana of a palace she and her family had once visited in Southern Spain. Then a flash of inspiration led her to realise that the palace garden had been based on gardens like this in ancient Rome.

The great man was seated on a marble bench with the young boy standing at his side. He indicated towards two other benches either side of him and Sextus, Sion and Briana sat down. The young boy also sat down but Aristophanes stayed standing.

When he noticed them looking at the standing Greek man, the man indicated towards Aristophanes and said, "I trust Aristophanes with so much but he is still my slave and therefore will stand but when I am dead he will be made a freed man in my will."

He looked back at Briana and Sion and asked "do you not have slaves in Britannia?"

Sion shook his head. "Not where we come from Consul."

The great man noted the use of his title rather than name and decided to act.

"I am Consul Gaius Marius and you may call me Marius. Aristophanes you know by name already but the boy you do not. He is my wife's, brother's son and is called Gaius just like his father, Gaius Julius Caesar. You may refer to him as Gaius."

Briana started at the name, looked at Sion who nodded and then looked back at the boy, who suddenly took on a more interesting aspect.

Marius continued "Lucius Sextus I know already as a reprobate from the Subura, who has been useful to me in the past but apart from the fact that you are from the remote island of Britannia, I know nothing of you two, let alone your names."

Sion took this as an invitation to speak. "Back in the lands we come from I am known as Sion ap Rhys and this girl is Briana ap Ysabel. Here I adopt the Roman style name of Sharnus."

Marius nodded his agreement.

"We are merchants who have brought goods from our home land to Rome and seek to learn more and study Rome, before returning home with goods and information."

Marius looked pleased at this. But waited as food and drink were brought out to the group. Briana was once again offered wine and this time olives were also available.

Marius continued. "You have come at a time of trouble for Rome. The city is in peril, not from outsiders but from dissenters inside the city who do not like the way that others are running the city. These *boni*..." he used the word with much venom "...are stuck in the past and don't understand that Rome has to change to survive. Otherwise we will fail just as Troy, Athens and Carthage have fallen before us."

"I think you have also come at an opportune time." He looked towards Sextus. "You Sextus, can give me information on what the head count are thinking about Marius, Sulla and a possible civil war."

He then turned to Sion. "And you Sion ap Rhys..." Sion nodded at the Celtic form of his name "...you can give me the picture from outside Rome. You are a trader, you have travelled through lands that most Romans have never even heard of, let alone dreamed of or visited. You can help me to understand what we need to do and where we can look to for help or conquest."

He indicated towards a door and they all got up to follow him.

However he turned towards Briana and said, "this is no time for children, you can stay behind."

Sion interjected. "Consul the girl must stay with me, I promised her family."

Marius waved away the request. "Nonsense, Rome is still safe and she will have my men to protect her, plus my nephew will show her some of the delights of Rome." Indicating towards the young Gaius Julius Caesar.

Sion looked worried but Briana had a big smile on her face.

CHAPTER TWENTY EIGHT

Morwenna was happy in her current environment.

Admittedly her first attempt hadn't managed to lure in the girl and Sion into the story she inhabited, as they had been diverted into another story, but she still felt that her powers would bring them to her eventually.

She was in a desert land. Her new body was powerful and she had already proved too strong for another of her kind, which had come to the same water hole as her.

She wanted the taste of human blood and from one family in particular but she would wait, she was good at waiting.

For now she would satisfy herself with the blood of something else, she headed off on all four legs to see what she could find.

CHAPTER TWENTY NINE

It was quite cold as Ysabel got slowly out of the taxi. She could see the steam form as she breathed out into the cold air. She spent a little time playing with puffing out in different ways, making pretty patterns in the cold night air.

I'm not drunk – she told herself.

Ok, maybe a little tiddly but not proper drunk.

She walked steadily and deliberately through her gate and up the garden path, making sure that she walked straight and wasn't going to weave at all. By concentrating so much on walking straight, she over-compensated and stumbled onto the lawn. She quickly regained her composure, returned to the path and looked around to make sure no-one had seen her. There was no-one in sight but the act of checking all around her, left her a bit spinned-out and in a bit of a head fuzz.

She breathed in deeply again and once again played with the patterns her breath made in the cold air.

"Right. Let's get in the door." She thought to herself.

She sought the right key from the multitude on her key ring and turned the search into a little game until it took longer than she had hoped, so she got frustrated, dropped the keys and had to start again. Finally she found the right key and tried to enter it into the key hole, after a couple of unsuccessful stabs she thought to herself. "Why doesn't someone create a front door that unlocks and opens when you press a button, like on a car door?"

"I'll create one!" she declared out loud, as the key slipped into the keyhole and turned to open the door. Ysabel stumbled through the door, didn't quite fall over, managed to regain her feet and looked around as if to say "I'm alright", realised she was on her own, smiled and closed the door behind her.

She headed into the kitchen to grab a glass of water, drank it quickly (with some dribbling down her front) and refilled. Then staggered back into the hallway and very, very carefully started walking up the stairs. Sometimes when you've had a few too many to drink, the steady walk up the stairs seemed to take an eternity. When Ysabel reached the top she thought there was one more step, tried to walk up it, found it wasn't there and stumbled head first into the wall in front of her.

"Shhh Shhh Shhh!" she said to herself, as she just managed to keep the water from spilling.

She made her way into the bathroom, turned on the light and looked at herself in the mirror and said "Oh god!"

She quickly finished her ablutions and walking past Briana's door, was about to open it to check on her but stumbled again.

"Probably best to leave her sleeping tonight, I'll see her in the morning." She whispered to herself before "shushing" herself once more.

She stumbled into the bedroom, managed to take off most of her clothing before crumpling up on the bed and falling straight asleep.

CHAPTER THIRTY

At first Gaius didn't looked pleased to have been saddled with Briana but Briana quickly learned that the young Caesar boy was nothing if not artful.

"It is not part of my plan to let my Uncle know that what he wants, I want also. So I make it appear that I didn't want to spend time with you, when really I did."

Gaius seemed to be tall compared with some of the other Romans Briana had met and he lead them both off through the streets to the Forum Romanum, the main civic centre of Rome.

Gaius wanted to listen to some of the advocates practicing on the Forum steps but he also wanted to listen to Briana. Briana for her part was overwhelmed by the sights on display. Everywhere she looked, something was happening.

There were priests gathered around a stone table examining something in detail.

Another man standing up on a small dais, was repeatedly talking about events. After a short while, Briana realised he was the newsreader of his day. People would stop and listen and then move on again when they had got the information they needed.

Carters carried their wares through the Forum on horse drawn carts or hand drawn versions. Some stopped to sell the wares when asked to do so by the potential customers, whereas others seemed intent on getting from one side of the Forum to the other.

The buildings mostly gleamed of white marble but some were looking more run down than others. Around one building there was a hive of activity and Briana watched as the men (there were few women in the Forum) brushed and cleaned the walls and floors.

Gaius caught Briana's eyes, followed her gaze and explained. "The temple of Castor and Pollux, it was in a terrible state and being used to house cattle, so my Uncle told the priests to sort it out immediately or incur the wrath of the gods!"

Briana nodded and continued to look around the Forum at the multitude of sights to behold.

Gaius bought a couple of half oranges from a man who was selling them from a tray, which was fixed around his waist and suspended from his neck.

"Here" said Gaius handing Briana one of the halves of orange. "Fresh oranges, you have probably not had them in Britannia before."

Briana was about to say that of course she had, when she realised where and when she was and kept quiet.

Gaius continued. "It is about Britannia, I wanted to talk to you."

He waited for Briana to comment but carried on talking when she said nothing.

"We know a lot about Near Gaul but less about Further Gaul and practically nothing about Britannia but I would like to think that Rome can have an influence over these places and I wondered what the people are like there."

Fortunately Briana had learned some things about Boudicca last term so she was able to speak with a bit more confidence than she would have done if they had not studied a little bit about the subject. She hoped that Boudicca's time wasn't that different to Caesar's. Little did she know or remember that Caesar would be the first Roman General to take an army over the English Channel into Britain and also that it was Caesar who would defeat the British Celtic relatives back in Gaul.

After explaining about certain things, Gaius asked specifically about the social structure over in Britannia.

"Our people are divided into tribes…" She paused for a moment, remembering something her Mother had told her "…and my tribe is called the Dumnonii, who are based in the South-West of Engl…" she caught herself "…South-West of Britannia."

"Each tribe is ruled by a chieftain and his wife and also by the Druids who are the priests, heal the sick and create the poems and songs for the tribe."

Gaius nodded his interest and for Briana to continue.

"We do not have the technology of Rome but our people fight with bravery and honour and while we fight amongst ourselves, we would also fight any attempt from outsiders to conquer us."

Gaius smiled at the passion which started to come through his young friend's voice as she said these last few words.

"And how do your people fight, Briana?" asked Gaius

Briana remembered the pictures she had seen and said "in chariots and both men and women go to war."

"I imagine that they are very brave but unruly. I am afraid they would be no match for the might and organisation of the Roman legions." Gaius observed.

Briana would liked to have said more in defence of her countryfolk but unfortunately she knew a bit of his history, so she kept quiet.

Gaius continued to ask more about Britannia but Briana realised that her history lessons had actually taught her little which would be of use in a conversation with the very inquisitive Roman boy who sat before her now.

She found herself floundering, making things up and trying to deflect Gaius as best she could.

She did remember a visit to an Iron Age Village which did help her explain a little bit more about the way of life, eating habits and family life, which Gaius found very interesting.

"You have been very informative Briana, I think it is very important for us Romans to understand the ways of the people who live around us. It helps when we come to bring them into our Republic."

Briana looked at him questioningly. "Why does Rome want to conquer everyone around them Gaius?"

Gaius in turn looked surprised. "We seek only to ensure that other people benefit from our ways as much as we do. Roman civilization is the epitome of order and modern thinking and everyone in the world should benefit from it and the guidance of the Senate of Rome. Sometimes people and nations don't see this, so we have to give them a little forced encouragement but everyone accepts Roman ways in the end."

He almost looked like he was talking to an audience as he spoke and a few people walking by did stop to listen to this aristocratic young man for a moment before moving on. Perhaps this power of rhetoric was one of the things which was to make Gaius Julius Caesar great. Again Briana wished she knew a little more about this famous man from history. She actually found herself thinking about nipping out of The Book, reading up on Caesar's later life and coming back in again.

However she was interrupted in her thoughts by the sounds of a sudden tumult from just outside the Forum. People were shouting and then others started running from one of the side streets.

Some of them were shouting too but Briana couldn't make out what they were saying over the cacophony now playing around the Forum.

One man ran towards them and Caesar cried "Stop" with such a note of authority that the man stopped immediately and many others also took notice.

"What is happening, friend?" asked Caesar of the man.

The man looked flustered but replied "Sulla is coming. He has crossed the pomerium and is marching into the city! He is hot on our heels and will be here very soon."

Gaius looked concerned but did not sound it when he continued to question the man. "Now take your time and think, is it just Sulla and his retinue or does he have his legions with him?"

The man looked like he wanted to run but still he stayed and answered this commanding young man. "He has six legions with him but he is coming ahead with a small band of men."

Gaius looked at him and said "you may go."

The man looked relieved and made his way off through the crowd. Many of whom were also deserting the forum.
Gaius turned to Briana "We must leave. Sulla will head for the Forum first and if he finds us...me, he will be very interested in my safety." Gaius gave Briana a look that they both understood.

At that moment the sound of marching men came from the same side road and then appeared a small cohort of men surrounding a man on horseback.

His blond hair made him stand out from the crowd, even if he had not been on a horse. He looked around the forum intently as if he was searching for something.

As he did so, his head moved showing off the scar down his cheek.

Gaius said "Sulla!"

Briana said "Cutwulf!"

Suddenly the blond man's eyes looked their way, widened with understanding and he leaned down to speak to one of his soldiers, pointed and they started to head towards Gaius and Briana.

Gaius looked at Briana. "We must go. NOW!" With that he lead Briana off towards one of the side streets while the Roman General and his soldiers headed towards them.

CHAPTER THIRTY ONE

How is it, that every time you have a hangover, you seem to leave the curtains slightly ajar and the early morning sunshine seems to manage to stream through, right into your face?

Ysabel thought this as she opened her eyes into bright sunshine, raised her head and instantly regretted it. If you are too young to have experienced a hangover yet, firstly you are lucky and secondly ask someone older to explain this bit to you properly!

Drinking that much wine seemed like a great idea last night but this morning Ysabel was paying for it, big time. Her head was pounding and her throat felt like someone had been up on to Dartmoor, got a bit of gorse bush and dragged it along the inside of her throat.

She did not even like to think what she looked like.

The sun streaming through the window indicated that it was probably time to get moving, even if it was a Saturday and a quick glance, which ended up taking a little longer as her eyes adjusted to looking properly, at the clock showed that it was indeed time to rise.

Ysabel sniffed the air, hoping to get a scent of the tell tale aroma which meant that Briana was up before her and got the coffee going in the cafetiere for her. Unfortunately no smell was permeating up from downstairs. Damn the girl, she thought.

She quickly re-thought that, as Briana was actually very kind to make her coffee in the morning but right now she really needed one.

She shuffled out of bed, like a creature from a zombie movie, made her way into the en-suite, stood in front of the mirror and then opened her eyes. She quickly shut them again, as the creature in front of her couldn't really be her, could it?

She looked again, decided it was her but she was not looking her best and turned on the tap in order to throw some water into her face. This did seem to help, so she repeated the procedure before towelling off, putting on a dressing gown and heading downstairs.

The kitchen showed no sign of habitation from Briana this morning, so she proceeded by herself.

Ten minutes later she was slightly refreshed after juice, coffee and pro-biotic drink and soon she was heading back upstairs with another coffee for herself and a first for Briana.

She knocked on Briana's door. No reply.

She knocked again, slightly louder. Still no reply.

She knocked once more and said "Briana, coffee!" Nothing.

She knocked again, loudest of all, saying "Briana, coffee" and walking in.

The bed was unused and The Book lay on top of the bed open.

Briana had obviously entered into The Book and been gone since yesterday evening.

Ysabel quickly put down the drink and went to The Book to see what was displayed.

She read quickly. "Reptile-like Monsters. Oh my god. What has Briana done?".

Without any other thought, she placed her hand heavily onto the article and was absorbed.

Her surroundings changed immediately, as she entered into a desert-like scene with rocky outcrops. The sand and rocks were almost blood red in colour.

There seemed to be very little vegetation and what there was, was stunted and scraggy.

There also seemed to be a bad smell but not all of the time, it seemed to come and go.

She was in a valley of sand with the red rocky outcrops on either side. She peered down the valley but it twisted in both directions, so Ysabel couldn't tell what was around the corner.

One thing she was sure of was that there was no sign of Briana or Sion.

She decided to brave a shout. "Briana...SION"

She waited as her call echoed through the valley.

The folly of shouting out when she had entered into a section called "Reptile-like Monsters" was not lost on Ysabel but she was not sure what else to do, so she tried again. "BRIANA!....SION!"

She waited once more, but still no reply or action of any kind. Which was good because she had not so far attracted the attention of the monsters but it was also bad as there was no obvious sign of Briana and Sion.

She decided to head off down the valley to see if she could locate them.

After about twenty minutes of walking she could finally see out of the valley on to a low plain, made up of more of the straggly undergrowth, red rocks and red sands.

However there was still no sign of Briana, Sion or the eponymous Reptile-like Monsters. The latter surprised her as it made no sense to have a section in The Book on something and then fail completely to make them available.

While their absence was a positive thing at the moment, she couldn't help wondering "where were the monsters?"

CHAPTER THIRTY TWO

The cause of Ysabel's confusion had just finished off another beast.

Morwenna the Gorgonopsid was a terrifying beast. She was the size of a small rhinoceros but with a body somewhere between a powerful dog and a reptile. Her species had been the dominant predator around 260 million years ago.

Her powerful jaws crushed the femur of her latest conquest.

While see was not here to destroy other gorgonopsids, she couldn't help having a little bit of fun while she waited for the humans to arrive.

The prone male gorgonopsid had been bigger than her and a worthy opponent but ultimately he was no match for her guile and determination.

She started to devour the flesh of the recumbent beast, the redness of the flesh matching the red markings on the back of her neck where her red hair would have been.

She quite liked this simple life, being an apex predator and, so far, the apex of the apex predators in this area. As well as her fellow gorgonopsids, she had been enjoying her roaming life by killing off some of the other megafauna that lived around here.

She had particularly enjoyed terrorising a group of bradysaurs which had stumbled through in search of vegetation. Though their tough hide and scales had proved a challenge she had enjoyed playing cat and mouse with them.

Whenever she needed to eat she had found one of the bradysaurs a perfect morsel to keep her going. Water had proved slightly harder to find but as she had begun to think more like an animal, she had begun to use all of her senses more and could almost taste the water on the wind, which led her to a few scrubby water holes.

She lifted her head from the body of her fellow gorgonopsid and despite the strong smell and taste of blood around her, she could sense something new in the air.

She moved away from the gorgonopsid and sniffed again. This was something new, something she hadn't smelled in the time she had been residing in this late Permian landscape. It suddenly dawned on Morwenna what the smell was, it was human scent.

Intrigued and just a little bit excited, she headed off towards the source of the smell.

CHAPTER THIRTY THREE

With the sound of hoof beats and running footsteps right behind them, Gaius and Briana headed off into the alleyway, the young Roman boy taking the lead. Ducking and diving from alleyway to alleyway.

Briana was impressed that her young friend seemed to know exactly where he was going. As to Briana it seemed that they were running through a labyrinth. Gaius seemed to take every new direction with confidence which indicated that his young years belied the knowledge he had already built up of the city.

Every time they turned a corner or passed through a group of people, they gained a little bit on the horsemen behind but in every clearer and straighter section, the horsemen had the advantage. If they didn't do something, it wouldn't be long before the two were caught.

They turned a corner and headed down a long, straight alleyway with large wooden doors on either side. After running about halfway, Briana looked over her shoulder to see the men on horseback catching them quickly on the long straight section. They would catch the two of them long before they reached the end of the alleyway.

The sound of hoof beats started getting louder and louder, Briana felt that the men would be upon them in seconds. She looked over her shoulder and could see Cutwulf just behind another horseman looking on with much excitement in his eyes.

The other horseman pulled a short spear from his side, weighed it in his hand once or twice, before raising it above his shoulder, ready to throw.

Briana screamed out "GAIUS" as the horseman pulled back his arm.

Gaius also looked over his shoulder with fear.

"Quick in here" he shouted and veered quickly to a slightly ajar wooden door on his left.

They ducked through into a small warehouse and heard a clatter as the spear hit the alleyway just where they had recently left.

Briana and Gauis didn't stop to see what was happening behind them and made their way through the warehouse, running past people loading fruit and vegetables into crates. The men doing the loading barely stopped to take any notice of the sudden intrusion.

The two youngsters looked over their shoulders once more and couldn't see anyone in sight. The horsemen must have reached the doorway but not been able to get through while still on horseback.

As they reached the end of the warehouse, they heard a crash behind them which answered their thoughts. Sulla and his men, now on foot, came crashing through the doorway and headed towards Briana and her young friend. However the disruption had given the two of them a valuable lead, as they exited the warehouse back into the warm sunlight.

Again Gaius led them, going one way and then another. They could still hear the men behind them but once again Gaius took a sudden sideways turn, this time into someone's house, waving and smiling at the lady of the house as he did so "Ave Cordelia" he called and she replied "Ave Gaius."

They emerged once again in to the streets which quickly got narrower and dirtier and the sounds of following men seemed to get lighter and then disappeared all together.

Briana was beginning to feel sick from all the running and was getting a stitch too but Gaius showed no sign of slowing down until they turned into another more crowded street and he suddenly slowed to a walking pace.

"Act normally and follow me" he instructed Briana in a slightly hoarse and gasping whisper.

Briana was happy to have stopped running but began to wonder where they were heading, when again Gaius turned quickly into a building, Briana followed him up some wooden stairs to the first floor.

Gaius knocked and entered without waiting for an answer. A tired looking man was seated behind a desk, with scrolls all around him.

Gaius walked straight up to him and said, "you know who I am." It was a statement of fact rather than a question but the man answered nevertheless.

"Yes Gai-", young Caesar cut him off.

"Has my uncle Cotta a barge on the wharves right now?"

"Yes Gaius, he has two. One has just arrived and one is being laden ready for departure."

"Where is that one going and when?" Gaius asked. Briana was surprised that the Roman boy was not now gasping for breath like she was.

The man replied. "All the way to Ostia and it should be ready to go within the hour."

Gaius turned to Briana. "Excellent. I can take the barge to Ostia and then take a ship from there to safety."

He then turned back to the man behind the desk.

"Thank you Gracchus you have been very helpful, Caesar will not forget it."

Turning back to Briana once more he said "come Briana we must leave." With that he led them from the room, back down the stairwell and into the streets.

He seemed to have recovered fully from his running and led Briana with vigour through the alleyways. The area they entered seemed to be much more commercial than before, as they walked past workshops, warehouses and traders. Plus the smells seemed to be getting stronger.

Then they ducked down one more alleyway and suddenly were in the dock area of the city. The sounds of men working on the wharves were tumultuous and the smell was stifling.

Gaius led them directly to one specific wharf, left Briana behind and went to talk to the man leading the team who were loading goods on to the barge. Gaius seemed to be doing all the talking and the man just nodded his assent.

When complete, Gaius returned to Briana and took her hand. "I will leave you now Briana. I am heading to Marsala via Ostia, as I need to escape the clutches of Sulla who is after me. You will be safe once I have gone."

Briana looked worried and stuttered "B-but..."

Gaius held up his hand to stop her. "Sulla has no quarrels with you, he will not recognise you without me. You will be safe, I swear."

Briana wanted to tell him all about Cutwulf and where he came from but didn't know how.

"Can't I come with you Gaius?"

"No. You must return to Sharnus, he will be searching for you. However, know that you have made a friend of Gaius Julius Caesar and whenever you return to Rome, look for me."

He looked over his shoulders to see the men had finished loading the barge and the team master nodded at him once more.

"Farewell Briana and bona fortuna."

They held forearms in the style of the warriors hand shake and then Gaius headed off.

He climbed up on to the barge which was pushed away from the wharf using long poles, the men then used the poles to punt the barge down the river towards the sea. Within a few minutes they were gone.

Briana was left standing on the wharf in a strange ancient city, suddenly feeling very frightened and very alone.

CHAPTER THIRTY FOUR

Sion was worried.

He had finally managed to get away from Marius under the pretense that Briana was his sister-daughter and he had promised his sister to look after her in Rome.

Marius had been loathe to let him go but then messengers had come to the great man and he had become otherwise occupied.

So now Sion had to locate Briana and take her back home.

Normally he could locate one of the family fairly easily within The Book. What he did was close his eyes and think strongly about the blood of Geraint. He wasn't sure exactly how it worked but he could usually then head straight towards where the members of Geraint's family were located. It had served him well many times in the past.

However this time the results were mixed and when he tried again (despite the strange looks he got from others in the street) the results were wildly different and pointing in a totally different direction and still seemed to be fluctuating.

What he couldn't know, was that he was actually not very far away from Briana and Gaius and as they ran hell for leather away from Cutwulf and his soldiers, their position in relation to Sion changed dramatically from being almost due North of his position, to due South.

The other thing that concerned Sion was that when he put his mind out to try and locate Briana, he sensed another more malicious mind too.

It took him a moment but he realised that Cutwulf was out there too.

He must find Briana and quickly before Cutwulf could find the girl. He dreaded to consider the possibility that Cutwulf had already located her and that was why his locating senses were disturbed.

CHAPTER THIRTY FIVE

The stillness was beginning to get to Ysabel. Every breath of wind was making her even more jumpy.

She should have been seeing Reptile-like Monsters but there was nothing there. The insecurity of not knowing where they were was even worse than locating them in her mind.

She expected them to appear at any moment but so far they hadn't. Up until this moment she had walked a couple of miles and now she was beginning to question her plan.

Of course, she could return back to safety but what if Briana and Sion were in danger in here and she was needed to help them?

Her mind was going crazy with dreadful possibilities for her daughter and Sion. She had a vision of them being attacked by the Reptile-like Monsters. That was the reason for the monster's absence, they were all attacking Briana and Sion.

She wasn't to know that the two of them were in a different section of The Book altogether. Also that the real reason for the quietness, was slowly making her way towards her.

Morwenna could sense that the human was nearby. It was funny how she was already beginning to think about "the human" as if she wasn't one herself. But after nearly 1000 years of inhabiting other creatures and environments totally alien to human beings, it was amazing how quickly you adapted to your current surroundings.

The stench of human sweat was drawing her nearer.

She was excited by the thought of drawing human blood but was it going to be the blood from one of Tristan's children?

That was important.

The smell was so intense now, she knew she was not far away. She could sense the human with her nose but wanted to see it with her eyes.

Ysabel had left the valley and the landscape opened up in front of her. At last she was able to see a wider variety of flora than had been in sight before. She could see a little woodland made up of what looked a bit like dwarf conifers.

In the distance she finally spied some creatures walking across the plain, they almost looked like a herd of cows. They weren't cows but she could now tell they lived a similar vegetarian life similar to cows back home as they had stopped to graze at some shrubs which adorned the side of the valley.

Perhaps these were the reptile-like monsters after all and there was little or nothing to fear from them. Her mood lightened a little. If she could just find Briana and Sion they could all head home and enjoy the rest of the day.

CHAPTER THIRTY SIX

The legionaries with Cutwulf knew better than to say anything. The children had escaped their clutches and their master would not be happy.

Why they were chasing the two youngsters, they did not know or ask, they did what their General asked them to do and the nature of their trade meant that they were often asked to perform tasks that many men would find strange or abhorrent.

Compared to some things they had seen and done, chasing a boy and a girl through the back alleyways of Rome was nothing.

There were now about twenty of them gathered in a group near the Circus Maximus. Their Centurion was talking to the General, who was talking very slowly and quietly. They had learned in their time with him, that this was not a good thing.

The Centurion was standing stock still as his General told him what he thought of him and his troops.

"Two children. Glavius. A boy and girl. Managed to evade you and your troops. Supposedly some of the best troops in the Roman legions and they cannot even run down two little children." He glared at the Centurion, who wisely said nothing, so Cutwulf continued.

"If they can't even catch a couple of little children, how in the name of Castor and Pollux are they supposed to cope with the screaming hoards of Pontus?"

This time he looked and waited for a reply.

The Centurion, taking the hint, replied.

"We will be ready General, we were just unlucky this time." He hoped this would be enough.

"Unlucky? Inept more like. I need those children Glavuis, they are paramount to the safety of Rome. Go and rejoin your slovenly troops, while I work on a plan."

Cutwulf enjoyed letting off steam in this way and exercising his power over his minions but it wasn't really the point of why he was here and he needed to get back on track.

Something had driven him to march on Rome sooner than the real Sulla had done. As if this change of tactic would somehow be rewarding.

So when he had marched into the Forum Romanum and spotted the girl of the line of Geraint, he knew that it was not just luck but some kind of destiny.

To then be frustrated in the simple capturing of the girl was annoying and confusing. He believed it was fated that he would get some revenge on those damned Britons which had cursed his life and haunted his waking thoughts. He was of the line of Woden and his ancestor would surely be wanting the best for his descendants.

He had to stop and think. If he could get over his anger he knew he could sense the girl and also see if there were any more of the British hiding within the alleyways of Rome.

He cleared his mind and pushed his senses out. The city was awash with conflicting emotions and thoughts but within it Cutwulf could sense a mind he had come across many times before, a Celtic priest who had been his nemesis on numerous occasions. Sion. The monk was North of Cutwulf's present position but on the move. Well, he could wait for now, Cutwulf had other targets to find.

He pushed his senses out once more and tried to concentrate on Geraint and his descendants. Nothing, he began to get frustrated but kept up his searching.

Ah. There it was. One mind in a sea of minds. Young, innocent and frightened. He smiled as he realised this. It was the girl and she was frightened. Scared about what Cutwulf would do to her. Cutwulf almost licked his lips in anticipation.

The girl was to the West. Cutwulf still didn't know the city well enough to know where that would lead but it was a start.

"Centurion, round up the men. We are heading in that direction." He indicated the source of mind he had sensed.

The girl was frightened and alone and Cutwulf was on his way to get her.

CHAPTER THIRTY SEVEN

Briana was indeed frightened. She was in a strange city with strange, foreign people. Although she could understand their language and they could understand her, they didn't really understand each other.

She had no money, didn't really know where she was or how to get back to where she had started from. When she had arrived with Sion it hadn't occurred to her to check where they were, as she had never really considered the possibility that they might be separated and Briana would be left to fend for herself.

She wasn't sure what she should do and where she should go. The obvious thing would be to try and find Sion. But where would he be and how would Briana find him?

Of course the last time Briana had seen Sion, he had been heading off in the retinue of Gaius Marius. He was supposed to be a famous man, so surely other people would know where he lived. So all she had to do was pluck up the courage to ask someone.

The only problem was that everyone looked too scary, too busy or both.

She was still in the dock area of the city and men were busy loading and unloading the barges which sat at the quayside. Other men were pulling hand drawn carts away from the docks laden with goods. There also seemed to be a lot of shouting which would make it difficult for Briana's young voice to be heard.

She decided to move away from the dock area and find somewhere a bit quieter, less busy and also where the people might not be quite so intimidating.

She headed down one of the alleyways and quite quickly turned left into a wider street. This area, only a few hundred yards away from the dock, was much quieter and more open.

She approached a brightly dressed lady but she scurried away as Briana got closer. So she tried a man standing in a doorway instead.

"I need to find the house of Gaius Marius" she asked the man who was dressed in a simple tunic but with an impressive leather strap over his shoulder.

The man, who had dark hair and deep, olive coloured skin, looked the girl up and down a couple of times before replying.

"And why would a young girl like you be after the Consul?"

"My friend is with him and I'd like to find them again but we got separated and I got lost." She tried not to sound too desperate.

The man took a moment once more before replying. "Come inside, I'll get my things and we'll go to Marius." He looked up and down the street as he said this.

Briana, knowing not to enter a strange man's house without someone with her, decided it was best to stay outside and said so.

The man looked like he was about to argue, then shrugged his shoulders before replying. "Whatever. Just wait here and I'll be back in a moment and we can head off to see the big man himself."

He headed through the doorway and was gone.

Something about his tone and manner disturbed Briana and she decided not to stay and headed down the wide road again, too frightened to talk to anyone else.

Just after she had turned the corner the man appeared once more. He looked up and down the street, shook his head and said "bloody young fool."

Not knowing that Briana had headed the other way, he himself headed off quickly in the other direction.

A short while later the man arrived at the villa of Marius and found the great man had already left but his steward was still there.

The steward explained that Marius had left when he heard that Sulla had entered the city. The new arrival then explained to the steward about Briana asking after Gaius Marius. On hearing this, the steward shouted down the hallway to a dark-haired man. "Sextus, who was that man and girl who were with you earlier?"

The dark-haired man turned and it was Lucius Sextus, friend of Sion, who replied "just a couple of Celts from Britannia petitioning the great man. Why?"

The steward replied, indicating towards the other man as he did so. "Publius Galvius here, found the girl wandering lost down by the docks but she ran away again."

"Glavius. Where did you see her?" Sextus asked the first man.

"Right outside my house Sextus." Glavius replied

The steward interjected "and I have heard word that Sulla is looking for Young Caesar and girl."

"Castor and Pollux!' said Lucius Sextus and headed for the door.

The girl in question, Briana, was even more lost than ever. She had been wandering around but wasn't quite sure which way she should head and so she had ended up nearly going full circle and was back by the river.

Suddenly a troop of soldiers came marching from a side street.

Not waiting to see if Cutwulf was with them or not, Briana headed hot footed away from them, over the nearest bridge and to the other side of the river.

Cutwulf could sense that he was getting close to the girl, he didn't even have to push his senses out any more, the girl was near.

At first he had sent the men off in the direction of his first senses but the streets ran in a different direction to the one in which he wanted to head, so he quickly became disorientated and confused.

So he had to stop and think deeply about the girl before he was able to follow again. Each time he had done this, his men would stand around idly wondering what their General was doing but not questioning him at all. This was the great Lucius Cornelius Sulla, the hero who had captured Jugurtha and poised to become the greatest man in Rome. So if he acted a little oddly at times, they would go with the flow.

But now Cutwulf had no need to stop and concentrate, his desired prey was getting closer and he began to think of what he would do to the young puppy.

The girl's family had denied him of his destiny to become one of the greatest warriors his people had ever seen. There would have been sagas written about him and he would have had the chance to be hallowed in Valhalla by Woden himself.

But that dog Geraint had cut short his life and consigned him to this "half-life" with no chance of reaching the Halls of Asgard. Yes, he could have some glory in this strange world but it was not the same.

He burned with a fire to end the life of the young puppy who was a descendant of the dog Geraint and gain some revenge. He was now closer to fulfilling his dream than he had been for some time.

"Keep an eye out for young Caesar and his girlfriend boys, I want to find them quickly" he called out to his men.

By the smell and the noise, he could tell that they were approaching the docks. They turned down another street and there was the River Tiber straight ahead of them.

Cutwulf motioned his men onwards and they continued to march down the street towards the river, all looking to and fro for any sign of the children.

Suddenly one of the legionaries called out. "General. Isn't that the girl over there, on the bridge?"

All of their eyes turned that way and Cutwulf followed the pointing finger to see Briana hot-footing it over the bridge.

"Well done, yes. Let's get after her boys!" And off they ran after Briana.

The sound of the running legionaries made everyone get out of their way, whereas Cutwulf could see that the girl's path was hampered by carts and people heading in the other direction over the bridge.

"Make way for the Consul Sulla!" The Centurion shouted at the crowds on the bridge but there was no need. The ordinary Roman people knew better than to get in the way of Roman Legionaries in a hurry.

They were catching the girl quickly. Hearing the noise behind her, the girl looked over her shoulder, took in the scene and looked horrified.

She was now over the bridge and headed to her left away from the line of carters making their way towards the bridge.

Cutwulf could see that the girl was heading towards the storage wharfs beside the river. With him and his soldiers making their way over the bridge, they would catch her up soon.

'Girl!" he shouted.

"I only want to talk with you" he lied and the girl looked again, this time into the face of Cutwulf.

He knew the girl could read his thoughts.

As the soldiers and Cutwulf continued to make gains on the girl, Cutwulf was delighted to know that it would not be long now before he was able to realise his dreams and make the girl suffer for what her family had done.

CHAPTER THIRTY EIGHT

Things were not quite going to plan for Sion. He had been trying to track down Briana but his senses were being distorted by a number of factors.

Firstly there was the presence of Cutwulf which seemed to be very strong at the moment, indicating that he was either very angry or very happy. Sion hoped it was the former.

Then also when he searched for the blood of the line of Geraint, not only did he sense Briana but from elsewhere in The Book, he sensed more minds stronger than they normally would be.

One was resonating even stronger than that of Cutwulf at the moment with an almost animal intensity. There were a few possibilities but his thoughts returned to Morwenna. There was also a mind very much like Briana's and that must be the Lady Ysabel.

What worried him most was that these two minds seemed intertwined in some way and he wondered whether Ysabel and Morwenna could be in the same section of The Book. He dreaded to think what Morwenna could do to Ysabel if she found her without him there to protect her.

He needed to find Briana quickly, get her away from the clutches of Cutwulf and then go and seek Ysabel and save her from the dreaded Morwenna if necessary.

He started to concentrate on Briana once more, trying to isolate her from the strong threads of the minds of Cutwulf, Morwenna and Ysabel.

Just then a voice called across the street to him. "Sharnus!"

He turned and there was Lucius Sextus striding towards him.

"Oh, Ave Sextus, I'd love to stay and talk but I need to find young Briana, she's gone missing."

The Roman smiled and replied "but that is why I have come to you, my Celtic friend. She has been seen asking for help down by the docks and my spies tell me that Sulla has arrived and is heading that way in search of young Caesar and that girl of yours."

Sion looked even more worried than before. If Cutwulf was to find Briana…he could not complete that sentence in his mind.

"Then you must help me find them Sextus, which way do we go?"

Sextus pointed and started to walk towards a side street. "This way to where she was last seen. If we move quickly it will not take us long."

The pair moved with determination. The streets were getting quieter as the news of Sulla's arrival started to permeate around the city.

Soon they were in the street where Briana had asked the man for directions before running away again. If only she had known that the man was a friend rather than a potential foe, she would probably be safe together with Sion once more.

Sextus indicated a building ahead of them. "This is where my friend Glavius met the girl but he does not know in which direction she made off."

Sion took this in and started to concentrate once more on the mind of Briana. This time it was much stronger and closer but he could also sense the girl's worry and fear, which was greater than he had experienced with her so far.

He could also sense the strong and hungry mind of Cutwulf which was coming from vaguely the same direction.

Sion knew exactly where to go now and he headed down a street and called to Sextus. "This way," making no attempt at explanation to the Roman on how he knew which way to go.

They both ran at some pace and soon were beside the river. Sion knew that both Briana and Cutwulf should be nearby here somewhere but where?

Briana's fear and Cutwulf's hunger had reached such new levels that Sion knew he must find the pair and now. Based on the senses that were coming through to him, they should be in front of him now.

But where the hell were they?

CHAPTER THIRTY NINE

Briana could see the soldiers gaining ground over her shoulder but unlike the alleyways where she and Gaius had escaped from them earlier, there were no nooks and crannies for her to try and escape. It was wide open now, on her left was the river and on her right a palisaded stockade about 40 yards from the river and there was no way through that palisade. All she could do was run straight down the middle of the two obstacles in clear sight of her pursuers.

The soldiers ran with determination behind her.

After a little while the stockade fence took a right angled turn so that it went right down to the river directly across her path, so there was no longer any way forward. Briana looked around for some way of escape but there didn't seem to be one anywhere. She was trapped.

Briana slowed to walking pace and looked over her shoulder. Seeing Briana slow down, the soldiers did so too and they spread out, each drawing their gladius (a Roman short sword) as they did so.

Cutwulf made his way through the middle of his men and then turned to speak to them.

"The girl is mine. Spread out and make sure she doesn't escape but leave her to me."

The men were already spread out but made an act of doing it even more, to show willing to their General.

Cutwulf approached Briana and stopped a few yards away.

"What is your name girl?" he asked.

Briana was almost too frightened to speak but managed to stutter "Br-br-iana."

Cutwulf continued "and do you know who I am?"

Briana gave a little nod.

Cutwulf smiled before adding, "then know it was Cutwulf who brought your life to an end and if you ever reach Valhalla, find Geraint and tell him that you are a present from me to him." He couldn't help but laugh.

"Now Briana be brave and take my sword like one of your ancestors and perhaps you will reach the Hall of Asgard."

He stepped forward sword in hand, ready to strike the blow which would end Briana's life, bringing him some revenge for the hurt her family had done to him over the centuries.

The girl was petrified and could not move, even to get away from the fatal blow which was soon to come.

Briana started to shake and cry, she didn't want to die.

CHAPTER FORTY

Suddenly the world she was in seemed a lot more pleasant to Ysabel, though of course she couldn't enjoy it as she was still distressed about the fate of Briana. However, you couldn't deny the beauty of the new surroundings.

There would be no grass for another couple of hundred million years but the valley had become much more verdant now with the dwarf conifers and ferns being the predominant plant life. This made the landscape less barren and much more welcoming. Also her hangover was beginning to recede and there was even a little waterfall.

As she was so thirsty now, she decided to try a little water, even though she knew the inherent risks of not knowing what was in it.

She needn't have worried, the water was refreshing and just what she needed. It was beginning to look like the perfect spot to bring Briana for a bar-b-q. Thinking about her daughter, brought back the reason why she was here in the first place. She had almost got stuck in the idea of following the valley and seeing where she ended up.

But now she started thinking about Briana and Sion again. She had seen no sight nor sound of them since she had been here and there now seemed a strong possibility that they were not here at all. A shiver went down her back and she started imagining the unimaginable again.

She decided to start heading back. On an impulse she called out one more time "Briana, SION!" The call rang out across the valley and beyond.

Morwenna lifted her head up at the sound of the call. Not only was that human, it was female. She had begun to sense her new prey was female but the voice confirmed it. It was also very close.

Although she was able to isolate the human woman by smell, the sound of the voice supported these instincts and she quickened her pace towards the source of the sound and smell.

Ysabel waited for a moment to see if there was any response to her call but all she could hear was the steady flow of the waterfall and the combined sounds of chewing, grinding of feet and the occasional fart from the large herbivores on the ridge, who were taking advantage of the verdant foliage to eat.

She was concerned that Briana and Sion weren't in here at all and after waiting for about a minute, she began the steady journey back to the way she had come into this world.

Suddenly a creature jumped out from behind a spur of rock into her path.

She had never seen anything like it before, not even on the television. It was at tall as she was and twice as long as it was tall. Its body was smooth and had a velvet-like sheen to it. However, what she was mainly looking at was the head and in particular the mouth, which was open and displaying a very healthy number of large incisor-like teeth.

Although she couldn't move her legs, as they were temporarily paralysed with fear, Ysabel was able to quickly look around her for a possible way of escaping the beast in front of her.

She was sure she had to escape. This was not a cosy, farting herbivore like the grazing animals on the ridge, the teeth gave this creature away as a flesh-eating carnivore. Also it seemed to be giving her a very malign look.

The way in front of her was blocked by the beast. Behind her, the way was open but showed no obvious possibilities of getting away. In her mind she could tell that the beast would be quicker than her on land and she didn't really want to risk trying out this hypothesis.

On one side was the steep incline of the ridge which did not give any obvious means of escape. What remained therefore as a possible means of escape was her left side which included the little waterfall and a pile of rocks, this way she felt, would be easier and quicker for her to scale than the beast would manage. The only problem was that she was now some 40 yards away from the rocks and she was not sure she would reach the potential escape route in time.

The beast followed her gaze and to Ysabel's astonishment spoke to her with a growly voice.

"You would not make it in time. These legs have such power, that I would be on you in seconds and you would be dead before you reached those rocks."

Ysabel just stood open mouthed in shock.

So the creature continued. "You did not expect me to speak did you Daughter of Tristan? You thought I was just another dumb creature like the others in this world."

Despite the imminent horror of being mauled, Ysabel was paying attention to what was being spoken to her and questioned the last statement. "Daughter of Tristan? My father was called Gryffyn. What do you mean?"

"You are descended from Tristan my brother, who was weak but still my father's favourite. I killed my father and would have had to kill my brother too if necessary but I was destined to fail and end up in here in this book for all eternity." Somehow she managed growl out this last statement even more.

Sudden realisation dawned on Ysabel. "You are Morwenna?"

If it was possible for a gorgonopsid to nod, then Morwenna did just that.

CHAPTER FORTY ONE

Sion had reached the River Tiber but couldn't see Briana. Everything was telling him that the girl should be in front of him now but apart from a few empty barges there was nothing to indicate there was a small, British girl around here somewhere. He looked both ways but apart from the normal goings on for the harbouside there was no sign of young Briana.

He turned to Sextus and spoke to the Roman. "I know you won't understand how I know but the girl should be here and now. We Britons can sense each other and my senses are telling me that she should be right in front of us now."

The Roman didn't look fazed or confused by this comment and said "right, let us find her now."

They started by looking around them in the street, first left and then to the right but there didn't seem to be any obvious hiding places. Some of the stevedores around them looked at the two men questioningly, as they seemed to hunt for nothing.

However strange happenings were common place at the docks of the most connected city in the world. Something new didn't bother them much, so they went about their business.

The two men then started searching the barges for any hiding places but it didn't look likely. The ones directly in front of them were simple open vessels used for carrying bulky cargo and did not provide much of a possibility of sheltering the young Briton out of main view.

"Are you sure the girl is here?" Sextus hadn't questioned Sion's feelings until now.

Sion pushed out his senses once more and was sure the girl was here close to them now and was possibly even more afraid now than when he last connected to her senses.

He began to worry that the child was actually lying dead at the bottom of the river and what he was sensing was the last thoughts and fears of Briana before Cutwulf had done away with her. When suddenly Sextus cried out.

"There she is, with Sulla!" He was pointing across the barges to the other side of the river, where plainly in view was Briana standing with Cutwulf closing in on her with a short sword.

Sion was paralysed with fear. It would be a matter of seconds before Cutwulf would do his worse and the girl would be dead. He could see Briana was cornered and had no support or means of defending herself.

He could think of nothing else but to shout across the river. "Briana!"

Briana took a moment to locate where the sound had come from, she looked back over the river towards Sion and Sextus in terror and began to cry even more.

Cutwulf looked on at Briana and then over the river to Sion with glee and continued to inch closer, as if he wanted to savour the moment and make the girl, and now Sion too, suffer as much as possible before he made the fatal blow.

Sion looked on in anguish. Then an idea came to him, why hadn't he thought of it straight away?

He shouted out across the river once more. "SWIM Briana. Swim across the river to us!"

He could see Briana looking at him in confusion.

So Sion shouted out again. "Jump into the river and swim to us Briana, you can do it."

Suddenly realisation seemed to dawn on the young girl. She threw off her outer garment and shoes and ran towards the river.

Realisation then dawned on Cutwulf too and he sped up, arms outstretched shouting "NOOOO!"

But he was too late, as he began to close on the girl he saw her leap from the riverside and dive straight into the River Tiber and was up almost immediately doing the front crawl.

Cutwulf was rooted to the spot, his own fear of swimming prevented him giving chase, so he called over his shoulder at the soldiers.

"Quick men, get after her."

The legionaries seemed confused and unsure what to do about this command. They seemed to be being asked to dive into the River Tiber after a young girl.

Cutwulf's face burned with anger.

"One thousand denarii to whoever catches her!" He screamed.

This fired the men into action, that was ten times what any of them would earn in a year. Those who could swim started stripping off any easily accessible outer garments and weaponry before diving into the Tiber after the swimming young British girl.

Briana however was already fifteen yards away and making use of her swimming skills to dodge the few vessels which were on the river and started to swiftly make her way across.

It looked like the girl would outstrip the soldiers, as they were not as talented as she was and they were also encumbered by slightly heavier attire. However just as she was pulling clear another barge came straight across her and stopped her progress completely. Briana started to tread water but found it hard in the wake of the barge.

When the barge had got out of her way, Briana started swimming again but her progress had been seriously interrupted. Although the majority of the soldiers were still floundering some way behind her, two were now much closer and one was closing quickly.

As she was looking over her shoulder at the oncoming legionaries, a small skiff suddenly came from nowhere alongside Briana and crashed into her side pushing her under the water. She re-emerged gasping for air, now with the lead legionary just yards away. The skiff had stopped and was still impeding her progress towards the jetty, so Briana, still a little disorientated, started swimming sideways to get around it.

This made the distance between Briana and her pursuer even shorter and the legionary thrust out his hand trying to grab Briana's ankle. Briana kicked her legs in fury either trying to get away or catch the man a glancing blow but unfortunately didn't quite succeed in either.

The man lunged once again, this time he managed to grab Briana's ankle and started dragging the girl towards him. Briana who had been beginning to flounder with all the effort, managed to find some hidden strength from somewhere and started kicking her legs with fury.

The legionary continued to hang on tight despite the thrashing legs of Briana but, as he pulled the girl closer to him, suddenly took a blow from one of Briana's feet right into his face. He reeled from the blow which had drawn blood from his nose and also seemed to have caught his eye. He let go of Briana's ankle and flung out his arms in anguish, managing to catch in the face the next soldier who had just managed to get alongside and was just making his way to try and catch Briana.

Both soldiers had now stopped swimming and were clutching their faces in pain.

Briana, no longer encumbered but nursing a sore foot from where it had caught the soldier in the face, resumed her swimming towards the bank. The way was now clear again and she could see Sion and Sextus waiting for her on the approaching jetty.

Cutwulf watching from the other bank, had seen all this with dismay, followed by delight, then anger and started to stamp his feet and shake his fists in frustration.

"Damn the girl" he shouted, as he watched Briana use her swimming skills to reach the other side of the river ahead of the soldiers and clamber onto the jetty aided by Sion and Sextus.

Cutwulf continued to scream. "And damn you lazy good for nothings." He turned on the soldiers who had not jumped into the river and started slashing wildly with his sword.

The legionaries knew the lay of the land and quickly hot-footed it away in the other direction.

On the other side of the river, having got Briana out of the water, Sextus was leading her and Sion away from the dockside.

He led them quickly down one street, turning quickly into another and then changing direction once more.

Briana stumbled on almost in a trance with Sion trying to support her shoulder. She was soaked through, was nursing one sore foot where it had connected with the legionary, was in shock and her feet were beginning to hurt without any shoes on. She stumbled and fell over.

Sion called out "Sextus wait. The girl cannot run any further."

Sextus turned back. He and Sion lifted Briana to her feet and between them arranged Briana so that Sextus could give her a piggy back.

"Now you just hold on tight young lady and I will get us to safety." Sextus called out over his shoulder and quickly started out once more as if there was no child clung to his back.

Sion looked over his shoulders but there were no sign of the soldiers. However he knew they had to get back to safety quickly because Cutwulf was still close and even more angry than ever. Plus he was worried about Ysabel being confronted by Morwenna elsewhere in The Book.

The swimming soldiers, on reaching the bank, made a perfunctory search of the nearby streets and alleyways. However, seeing their quarry had disappeared and their master was gone from the other bank, the soldiers decided to head along to somewhere they could get dry clothing and something to eat and drink.

The tall legionary who had got so close to catching Briana, before the girl's flailing foot had caught him in the face, led the group, nursing his bloody nose and blackened eye. The group were wet through and disconsolate. The denarii prize would not be theirs today.

CHAPTER FORTY TWO

Morwenna the Gorgonopsid almost smiled as she continued to growl out "Ah, so you have heard of me then child." She called Ysabel child even though, in actual years of living on the earth, Ysabel was the older one of the two and in fact, old enough to be Morwenna's mother.

She replied "yes, my father spoke about you to me and so did Sion."

"Silence!" Morwenna thundered. "Do not speak of that impotent priest. One day I will find him again and end his life." She almost seemed to smile or bare her teeth. "But for now, you will do."

She suddenly darted forward and opened her mouth in milliseconds and took a scraping bite out of Ysabel's leg.

Ysabel cried out in pain and crumpled to the ground, clutching her leg which started to bleed.

Morwenna didn't pounce again immediately, she seemed to want to savour this and she started to strut around Ysabel and snarled once more. "Does that hurt? I will make sure you feel more pain before I put you out of your misery, girl. My life has been but a shade of what it could have been in this book and someone should pay for this half-life that I lead." Uknowingly she mirrored Cutwulf's words with the term "half-life".

Again she darted forward. This time Ysabel managed to raise her arm but only succeeded in catching Morwenna's teeth down the length of her left forearm which now sported bloody gouges.

Once more Morwenna retreated to prowl and circle her prey. However this time Ysabel grabbed the initiative and picked up the hand-sized sandstone rocks which lay on the ground near to her, she then started throwing them at the prowling Morwenna.

Although she was in severe pain in her leg and left arm, her right arm was still in fine fettle. Her throwing was true and met with immediate success when a rock hit Morwenna squarely on the nose and brought a loud yelp from the symbiotic creature who now bared her teeth even more.

"So you have fight girl. Excellent, it is good to see the strong blood of our female line still burns with fire and strength. This fight will be more fun than I thought at first."

Once again she darted forward but Ysabel was quicker this time. She had started to learn that Morwenna would talk and then pounce so she was ready, rock in hand.

As Morwenna came in for the bite, Ysabel used the rock to crunch on the animal's cheekbone. Again Morwenna yelped but she also managed to swipe her claw at Ysabel's side and rip her clothing and tear at the top of her skin underneath.

Again she backed away and Ysabel clutched for rocks and threw them. A couple hit their target but Morwenna was also getting used to Ysabel's tactics and managed to dodge a couple of the throws.

A short spell of fairly unsuccessful fighting on both sides followed as Morwenna darted forward to be met with light blows and succeed in only lightly scratching Ysabel. In between, Ysabel's success with her rocks became muted as the beast successfully managed to dodge the missiles and stopped presenting the vulnerable parts of her body to be hit.

Another more pressing problem soon became apparent to Ysabel. She was running out of rocks.

She had exhausted most of the supply immediately around her. There were more rocks a few feet behind her but the injured leg meant that any move in that direction would leave her hopelessly open to attack from the rear by Morwenna and almost definite death.

A few more incursions and her supply was gone. She scrambled around with her hands in the dirt but none were forthcoming.

Morwenna appeared to smile once more. "You have proved a worthy opponent, what is your name?"

Ysabel automatically replied "Ysabel." Although she was not sure whether Morwenna would make any use of this new knowledge or not.

Morwenna, however, had no interest in using her name except in addressing her prey. "Ysabel, I am proud you are of my family and I will take great pleasure in sending you to meet your ancestors in the afterlife. Say hello to my brother and father for me and say I am happy once more."

She started to move forward slowly.

Ysabel tried to raise herself to her full height even though she knew she had no real response to the jaws and claws of the massive beast in front of her.

Morwenna got closer and and then steadied herself for the final pounce. She had grown to like Ysabel and with this in mind she had decided to end it now and quickly with one bite to the neck.

Ysabel knew there was nothing she could do but steadied herself ready for the attack.

Morwenna coiled her muscles and leapt.

But just at that moment, two other gorgonopsids came at her from either side and took her down in a mass of snarling jaws and slashing claws.

The two gorgonopsids, tired of the slaughter of their kind from this interloper female had decided to join forces and together take her down. They had followed her scent and increased their speed at the smell of fresh blood. Finding Morwenna there on the valley floor, they had waited and come at her in a pincer movement from behind the conifers, which meant that they were hidden until the last moment and were able to attack her undefended sides.

Ysabel spotted her window of opportunity and while the three gorgonopsids battled with each other, she dragged herself away out of harm's reach, further up the valley and back towards the way she had come into this world. She wanted to put as much distance as possible between herself and the monsters fighting behind her.

Back on the valley floor, the battle wasn't going well for Morwenna but she fought with determination. Up on the ridge the bradysaurs watched the struggles of their former tormentor and made a sound, which if they were human, you would have taken for laughing.

CHAPTER FORTY THREE

Sion, Sextus and Briana had reached the tavern belonging to Sextus once more.

Briana had been re-clothed in dry clothing and her foot was being tended by Sion, who was using essence of lavender and arnica to tend her swollen and bruised ankle and foot.

"Sextus" Sion said to the tavern owner. "We need to get going soon. The girl's mother is also in danger, so we must seek her out and help her."

Once again Sextus did not question Sion's knowledge of things which appeared to be beyond him.

"Of course my friend. I will come with you with as many men as you desire." He indicated to some of the people in his tavern. They looked like an unruly bunch but also with that innate strength and guile that Sextus also displayed.

Sion smiled. "Thank you for your offer Sextus but this will be one journey that only Briana and I can take. But I will see you in the future I hope, so we can work together once more?"

Sextus started to raise his hands at the rebuttal but seeing the earnestness in the monk's resolve, he acceded, saying, "of course old friend but is the girl strong enough to travel and aid you in your mission of mercy?" He nodded towards Briana lying on the wooden table.

Sion nodded. "I will take her to a safe place on the way and she will be safer there than anywhere here and now."

The sudden use of the temporal, didn't pass unnoticed with Sextus but he chose to ignore it.

He helped Sion to get Briana to her feet and they both helped the girl get used to walking once more.

At the crossroads just beyond the tavern, they took their leave of Sextus. The parting was swift, as Sion was wary of the need to help Ysabel. He could sense her feelings and she seemed to be in even more discomfort now than she had been before.

Although she was worn out, Briana was keen to get home and get to her bed, so gladly kept up with Sion as he led back through the streets of Rome.

"Is Cutwulf going to get us?" she asked of Sion.

Sion, who had been checking on the location of the Saxon periodically, answered "no, we are safe for now, he is still located in the area around the docks meeting out punishment to his men."

The two Britons headed back to the point where they had joined the Roman world and Sion held out a hand and they were both back in the pages of The Book once more.

"I cannot follow you now Briana but head back to your bedroom and I will seek out your mother."

Briana tapped on The Book once more and returned in a flourish to her bedroom. She put The Book up on to her dressing table, got into bed and, despite the worry about her mother, promptly fell asleep.

CHAPTER FORTY FOUR

Ysabel was unsure how far she had travelled originally to get to the place where she had been mauled by Morwenna but it seemed longer on the return journey.

Obviously that was partly due to the fact that she could barely walk but also she was worried that she had taken a wrong turning somewhere.

It had seemed so obvious on the way here, there seemed to be a natural direction to follow, that almost seemed like a pathway, perhaps the herbivores regularly used it like you found with cows or sheep back home.

However on the return journey she had already had two occasions where she wasn't sure which way to go and perhaps she had already gone wrong and was travelling round in circles or heading in completely the wrong direction.

When she had started out, she had felt relieved to be free of Morwenna but now she was getting worried again. What if Morwenna had escaped her two assailants and had set out to get her revenge on Ysabel at last? Or what if the two assailants had managed to overcome Morwenna and, driven by the bloodlust that the attack on her had fired up in them, decided to track down Ysabel as just desserts?

The amount of time she was taking to cross the land, combined with the possibility that she was going in the wrong direction would mean that any of them would soon catch up with her. Once caught, she would not provide much of a contest for any of them.

She decided to see what weaponry she could lay her hands on. She knew rocks were quite successful, as they had helped her already with her struggle against Morwenna but the problem was that they didn't last very long.

She decided to add some rocks and put them in her pockets but also seek out something else which she could use as well.

She looked around but the plants were of no use, nothing seemed to have the rigidity that she required, there were no nice woody trees, with perfect branches to use as staffs or clubs.

Then, at the top of a steep bank, she spotted the perfect thing. The skeleton of some long dead beast had been cleaned by predators and the elements and left a whole series of potential weapons for Ysabel to use. In fact she could spot the perfect thing, a femur had become detached from its adjoining bones and looked like it was about three feet in length and the perfect weight to make it very useful to her.

The only problem was the location, she would have to scale a very steep bank to get to the bone. Ordinarily it would be difficult but in her damaged state it would prove even more of a problem.

She debated whether to carry on and look for another weapon or even to escape from this world but the fear of being caught by one of the beasts and the close proximity of the femur, made it feel like too good an opportunity to forgo. She steeled herself to climb the bank.

It was a steep bank made up of hard stone which seemed to be covered in a dark gravel. As soon as she placed her feet on the incline, they slid down again.

Again she debated carrying on, when suddenly she saw cracks in the rock under the gravel. These cracks would provide hand and footholds to enable her to scale the incline.

She took the first tentative steps and was soon halfway up the slope. The next step would necessitate quite a large lunge with her right leg but she felt she could do it. Putting the weight on her left foot and hands, she took a couple of practice swings with her right foot before she thought she could manage the actual lunge up the slope.

With extra effort she lifted her right leg up, easily managed to find the foothold and now full of confidence lifted her left leg with the momentum she had begun with her right leg. However this time her foot did not manage to find its foothold and started to slide down the slope.

Her whole weight shifted and she moved one of her hands to regain her balance but found her downward impetus was too strong and when she tried to remove her right foot from the foothold, she found it was stuck.

She started to panic, her body twisted in the air as the left side slipped down the slope and the right foot stayed put. She could feel the pain in her groin and right ankle and suddenly as her body shifted once more, there was a crack as her right ankle gave way and she screamed in pain. All went black.

Sion knew his mistress was in danger but where was she?

He sent his mind out and tried to blank out the pain of Briana back in her bedroom and the anger of Cutwulf back in ancient Rome.

He could feel the pain and discomfort of Ysabel but it was interwoven with the fear and pain of Morwenna, which seemed confusing.

However, he could now isolate their location in The Book, so he found the right section, placed his hand on the page and entered into the Permian world which was home to the reptile-like monsters known as gorgonopsids.

He looked out on the barren world, just as Ysabel had done before him and he tried to isolate her, however her signals were weaker than ever. Could she be asleep? Or worst still, dead?

He followed his best guess and headed out into the wilderness.

Ysabel came to in a daze and immediately felt pain in so much of her body. Her ankle was hurting the most and was probably broken but she also had grazes from sliding down the rock face, together with the damage inflicted by Morwenna plus she seemed to have banged her head in the fall.

She was lying at the bottom of the slope in a heap and covered in dust and gravel. Her face was pushed into the ground and she had a mouthful of the aforesaid gravel.

She spat it out and tried to right herself but every movement caused her pain. She eventually managed to get herself into a seated position but the effort of raising herself up, made her feel very woozy and she almost passed out again.

She realised that she would not be able to move from the spot she was in, so decided to try and ready herself for the battle which was surely to come. Whether it was to be with Morwenna or the two other beasts or with some other, so far unseen, opponent she did not know but her current predicament was grave and almost totally without hope. She steeled herself for the fact that it was likely that she would die here in this spot, even if the attack did not come soon, she would probably not stay awake for long and would possibly die of hunger or thirst.

She got out her rocks and found what other ones were lying near by her and laid them out so that they were easy to access for when she needed them. She raised herself up as best as possible and waited.

And waited.

It was still light but she really feared it getting dark or her falling asleep.

At one point she started to fade and found her mind wandering. She came to her senses and pulled herself out of the oncoming fog in her mind.

I will fight like my ancestors before me. Perhaps I will get to fight with Morwenna once more and while I am unlikely to be successful, I will show her there is still fight in our family.

Presently, she heard a noise coming from around a nearby slope. Something was approaching. It sounded like a large thing based on the amount of noise it was making and she guessed that it was one of the large predators, as it seemed to have no fear about being heard.

She got the rocks ready and as the shadow and silhouette of the creature emerged around the slope she let loose with one of the rocks in order to take it unawares and try and gain the element of surprise.

CHAPTER FORTY FIVE

However what surprised Ysabel even more was that the creature which appeared around the slope was not one of the dreaded gorgonopsids but was in fact Sion. She watched in horror as the rock flew right at him but almost cried in relief as it sailed just past his right earlobe.

Sion shouted in alarm, ducked all too late and then looked for the source of the missile which would have done him much damage if it had hit its target.

He suddenly spied Ysabel lying on the ground and then blanched at the state she was in. He strode over quickly and called out to her.

"My lady. How are you?" he asked stupidly

Ysabel managed a smile. "I've been better Sion."

"Can you walk?" he asked with concern

"Let us see if we can try." She replied and then continued. "There are some dreadful beasts here Sion and one of them contains Morwenna, who is after my blood."

Sion continued to look concerned. "I know my Lady, I could sense her and your thoughts intertwined together. I think she is still not far away but weaker than before."

Ysabel nodded. "Yes, that would make sense. She was attacked by two more of her kind and when I left she was fighting a losing battle." She started to try and raise herself up.

Sion rushed over to help and aided her to her feet. One ankle was too sore to stand on, so she had to walk by leaning against Sion and practically hopping. Once more she began to swoon a little.

"Was it Morwenna who did this to you?" Sion asked as they hobbled along.

"Partly. She managed to get me with a few slashes of her claws and with her teeth as well but some of this I managed to do by myself. I tried to climb that ridge back there to grab a bone to use as a club." The thought of this jogged her memory as to why she was doing it in the first place.

"Sion. I'm worried that those beasts will come and get us, they were terribly violent." She shuddered as she said that and even the small movement she was making was painful to her.

"We are fine my Lady. When Morwenna was strong she was able to influence The Book and make this section unsafe for you to be in. Now she is weaker and I am here, we are safe once more. The Gorgonopsids may come close to us but they should not attack us."

He looked around. "However I think it would be good to get you back home, just in case."

Ysabel nodded her assent and they carried on at a speed amenable to her current condition.

The return journey took longer than her first journey and Ysabel realised that she must have been heading in slightly the wrong direction after all.

Despite the predicament they were in and the discomfort of Ysabel, at various points Sion pointed out things and described them, as if he couldn't stop himself. The herbivores turned out to be called bradysaurs. They were currently in the late Permian period. Which was also instrumental in creating a lot of the red sandstone and red soils that were famous in later Devon geology, agriculture and seaside tourism.

Ysabel listened vaguely and didn't have the heart to tell Sion that she didn't really care at this moment.

Soon they returned to their entry point and Sion activated the way back into The Book. When they were there, he helped Ysabel and they returned to the present day once more and found themselves in Briana's bedroom.

CHAPTER FORTY SIX

Briana was still fast asleep on her bed, even though it was obviously full daylight outside.

Sion laid Ysabel down on the bed next to her daughter and started to check on her condition and treat her. After a while he said, "no broken bones but your ankle is badly sprained and there are some very nasty cuts and grazes that will need treating straight away."

As if by magic, an apothecary set, a medical bag and a box of fresh herbs appeared next to him and he started tending Ysabel's wounds. He began by taking some linen, dipping it in water and crushing some herbs by hand and placing the combination together around Ysabel's ankle.

Ysabel winced and asked the monk "Sion, how are you able to leave The Book? I thought you were unable to do so."

Not stopping what he was doing, the monk replied. "The presence of you, Briana and The Book all in close proximity make it possible for me to be here for a while but not to go too far."

"What would happen if you went too far?"

Sion grimaced. "I would not like to try and find out my Lady. Suffice it to say I am able to help you here and now but I would not try to leave this room."

Ysabel nodded and then winced again as Sion tended one of the deeper cuts on the side of her torso.

"I think you will have to help me to get better Sion. I think any local hospital would not understand that I got these wounds from a 250 million year old carnivore!"
Despite the pain she was able to chuckle to herself.

"Yes my Lady. I am here to make you and Briana better."
Ysabel took the opportunity to look at her, still sleeping, daughter.

"What happened to Briana, Sion? Is she alright?"

"Yes my lady. She also had quite a run in, this time with Cutwulf..." at this name Ysabel started but Sion raised his hand and continued "...but there is no need to be concerned. She is much fatigued and has a slightly sore foot that should be better by the morrow. It could have been much worse but it was not. I will redeem you with the full details when you are fitter. Or possibly Briana will do it herself when she is awake."

He smiled at the thought.

"For now, I think you also need some rest." He had stopped tending to her wounds and began tidying up the tools of his trade. "I have finished for now, so I will leave you and Briana and let you rest. I will return to see you tomorrow."

He picked up his bits and pieces and looked back at the bed which now housed two sleeping residents. He silently returned to The Book.

CHAPTER FORTY SEVEN

When she awoke, Briana did indeed regale her Mother with the full story of her adventures. The story developed with her telling. The discussions with Gaius Marius lasted only a few seconds whereas her escape from the legionaries in the River Tiber became a veritable saga of attack, rebuttal and finally a close run escape from the clutches of evil.

Ysabel though tired and ailing, kept up with the story and gave support when needed. She was delighted that her daughter's swimming training had paid dividends but decided not to make an issue of it now. She planned to bring that up when both of them were fully recovered.

For her part, she only touched lightly on the events surrounding her own adventures, just alluding to getting into a scrape with some creatures when searching for Sion and Briana in another part of The Book. She did use the opportunity to give a little moral advice at this point.

"Of course this is why we should always be with Sion when visiting The Book, as he can protect us from any of the dangers which lie within."

Briana nodded in agreement, not wanting to mention at this point that she WAS with Sion, whereas her Mother had entered into The Book on her own.

Ysabel also decided not to mention the intervention of Morwenna at this point, as it would only concern her daughter and bring an added complication to her understanding of the machinations of The Book.

Ysabel was still not well enough to rush about the house, so Briana took it upon herself to go and make them breakfast, even though it was actually early evening.

Both ate heartily and were soon feeling drowsy once more. Sion returned to check on them both and gave them both a draught of a hot drink he had brought with him.

Briana found that the drink warmed her thoroughly and also it made her feel even more drowsy. After quickly tending over Ysabel's wounds once more, Sion covered them both up with the bedclothes and they were quickly asleep once more.

They both slept soundly for another fourteen hours and awoke at around 7am. Fortunately it was a Sunday so they had neither school nor work to attend.

Ysabel would be able to arrange to work from home for a short while and she would also let the restaurant know she was unavailable for a few days and this would help her to recover more, before having to face the real world. Briana's injuries were superficial and would go largely unnoticed when she returned to school on Monday.

They decided to stay in Briana's bedroom while Briana once again made breakfast. Over breakfast, they found they talked more than they had in many years. Sion came back and treated Ysabel's wounds again, while pronouncing Briana fit for active service once more.

Ysabel asked Sion about Cutwulf and the monk had to profess that he didn't know what had become of his old adversary.

"He is shielding his thoughts from me at this moment, so I don't know where he is or what he is doing."

Ysabel looked at him with concern. "Is The Book safe for us to use?"

Sion gave a slight resigned shrug and smile. "The Book is never completely safe but as I indicated before, as custodians of The Book, I think your family needs to continue to use it and keep that bond strong. Otherwise it could be used as an instrument of power by some hands or even worse, some of the elements which currently reside within The Book might be able to escape its confines once more and terrorise the modern world."

Ysabel shivered at this thought. She was pleased that Sion hadn't referred to Morwenna as she wanted to keep that whole episode from Briana for now. Although Briana was aware of Morwenna and some of the others in The Book, Ysabel felt that one evil character with murderous intent on their family was enough for her daughter to be thinking about at the moment.

Briana went back to school on Monday and this gave Ysabel the opportunity to chat to Sion, while he once again tended her wounds. She marvelled at his knowledge of different balms and remedies and wondered what a modern GP would make of his medical ministrations. One thing was for certain, her wounds were healing well. Yes, she would have scars where Morwenna the Gorgonopsid had gouged her but they were looking much better than Ysabel had ever hoped they would and she would be up and about much quicker than expected.

"So what of Morwenna?" she asked Sion as he applied a calendula and lavender balm to her thigh.

"I think she is still alive, if alive is the right word for what she has become. There are faint resonances of her malice still within The Book. I'm not sure if she has stayed in the same section or moved on now."

Ysabel nodded. "I'm still worried about using The Book but you seem to think we must."

Sion also nodded. "Yes. I am afraid you now have that obligation to continue to tie The Book to the blood of your family to prevent others from taking control. What I would recommend is short regular journeys which are accompanied by me and we will together tie The Book to us once more."

He looked at Ysabel.

"You, however, must take a rest from The Book for a while. Send Briana to me tomorrow and I will show her something nice and safe."

Ysabel looked slightly concerned but agreed. "Yes. I think she is a little bit wary about The Book once more following her experiences in Rome, so it would be good to start with something simple and less stressful!"

Sion finished his attentions to Ysabel and said "excellent. I look forward to seeing her tomorrow. And you, my Lady should return to your own bedroom tonight as a good night sleep in your own bed will help finish off your healing process."

Ysabel smiled and said "yes Doctor!"

Sion took a bow and disappeared into The Book once more. He had plans of his own and went off searching.

Later that evening, Ysabel had moved back to her own bedroom and managed to get Briana to change the bedclothes on her own bed. She even managed to get her to get the dirty washing sorted and was quite pleased with the progress she was making with her.

The recent events had definitely brought the two of them closer together, as both being threatened with their lives was a shared experience that most mothers and daughters didn't get to share with each other.

Briana cleared away the remnants of their supper from her mother's room, where they had shared their evening food together.

Ysabel looked at her daughter and said "Briana. Sion would like you to return to The Book with him tomorrow. Are you ready to return?"

Briana took a while to answer and Ysabel was concerned that she was going to be too frightened despite all her talk of bravado when escaping the pursuing legionaries.

"Yes Mum. I know all about it now. The Book is an important part of our family life and I have an obligation to it, to you, to Sion and to everyone out there." She waved her hand at the world in general.

Ysabel was proud of her daughter. Although her words were a little bit pompous, she knew that this was her daughter's way of dealing with the fear that was naturally stirring within her. So she could excuse a little bit of pomposity, though she would have to keep an eye on the television she had been watching to find out where she had been learning such pretty speeches from.

She hoped that Briana would be able to overcome her fear and interact with fun and adventure within The Book once more. She also hoped that she also would be able to do the same, once she was well enough to return.

One thing that was definitely for sure, she would not take The Book for granted any more.

"Ok. After school tomorrow, you can open The Book once more and wait for Sion to show you something that should be quite fun."

"Sure Mum. Good night"

Briana leaned over and kissed her mum on the cheek.

She returned this kiss and replied "good night my darling."

EPILOGUE

Morwenna was nursing her wounds, she had defended herself against the two gorgonopsid attackers but only just.

The effort had taken a lot out of her and she couldn't even raise her body to leave the world in which she found herself.

The recent escapade had knocked her, both physically and mentally. She needed to recover her strength and plan for the future.

Sion was more worried than he had indicated to Ysabel. The strength of Cutwulf and Morwenna had worried him, as they had never had that much control over the sections of The Book before. Briana and Ysabel had barely escaped with their lives and would probably bear the scars for the rest of their days.

He had to do something about it. One name came back to him, there was some confusion currently but at this moment, it was the best option that Sion had. He went off to chat to someone.

Cutwulf was also worried. Yet again, he had got close but failed in finishing off one of Geraint's family. He was strong, he had power and yet he kept on failing.

He hated to think about the idea, as he was so proud of his own strengths, but perhaps he needed some help.

Who would help him?

He sat down to think.

Briana left her Mother and returned to her own room. She got ready for bed and decided to move The Book from the edge of the bed, where it had been left, to the desk at the side of her room.

As she did so, she couldn't help fingering the spine and on impulse, decided to open The Book up.

She alighted on the double page spread and read the words aloud which first greeted her eyes.

"Reptile-like Monsters."

A glint came to her eyes.

"That sounds kinda cool"

She looked over her shoulder and raised her palm towards The Book, lowering it to the words on the page...

If you enjoyed this book, please
review it on Amazon Books.

You can also view other books on our website at
www.devonauthor.co.uk and follow the author
on Facebook - Simon Tozer - Devon Author

Printed in Great Britain
by Amazon

23429215R00121